New Leaves, Old Scars

Jennifer Drewett

Copyright © 2024 by Jennifer Drewett

All rights reserved.

No portion of this book may be reproduced in any form without written permission from the publisher or author, except as permitted by U.K. copyright law.

Acknowledgements

Sometimes, these acknowledgements are either too brief or too long. I'll endeavour to do my best to avoid both. I'll also make sure not to make it full of inside jokes you, the reader, will not understand. That's never a fun experience to read and I have a very clear invested interest in getting you to read my work.

To Alex, my wonderful partner since 2015 and my best friend. Your jokes make me smile even on my darkest days and your kindness shines even on the hardest of days. Your support throughout the writing process of each novel is just one of the things I treasure about you.

To my great grandmother Hilda Hill who the protagonist is named after. I know we didn't know each other properly when you were alive but you've been a bigger influence than you'll ever know.

To Mairon who gave me the title. He's also a brilliant writer in his own right. His book is called *The Octagon's Eight* by Mairon Oakley.

Content Warnings: familial estrangement, magic, supernatural peril, familial death, grief, serious injury, abuse of an employee, panic attacks, description of a dead body, disassociation

'New Leaves, Old Scars' is dedicated to all the neurodivergent people out there: this is for you.

Chapter One

Rays of sunshine shone through the astragal bar windows in the office, blooming over a young woman who sat behind the front desk. Her ashen hair, which was tidily placed in a ponytail, matched her monochrome office wear. She scribbled away into her multicoloured, worn-out notebook. A trickle of sweat slid down her nose as she focussed on the page in front of her. A fantasy world came to life from her imagination to her notebook as the seconds ticked by. The notes were scattered in their presentation, but she could understand what she was writing. She was absorbed in the process as the seconds ticked by to the sound of her approaching colleague's high heels. Hilda wrote of a witch walking along a disintegrated pavement, clacking in her heels as she walked. Hilda's colleague checked her watch as she stopped by the desk: it was 2:58 pm. She looked for an opening to grab the attention of the woman at the desk.

"Hilda?" the colleague spoke softly. Hilda continued to write. After a few seconds, the colleague huffed, hoping to grab Hilda's attention to no avail. She looked at her watch as it struck 3:00 pm. Impatient, she slammed her hands on the edge of the desk. This startled Hilda enough to break her focus. She dropped her pen on the floor. She faced her colleague in a fluster but avoided direct eye contact.

"Gabriella!" Hilda exclaimed.

"You weren't paying attention," Gabriella snidely retorted as Hilda picked up the pen. Hilda was angry but just wanted to escape the situation. Hilda grabbed her satchel bag, composed herself, and came back up from the floor with a fake smile strewn across her face.

"I didn't see you there, Gabriella," Hilda smiled, "I'll be up in a second." Hilda contained herself as she logged out of her office computer. She placed her notebook and pen hastily into her satchel bag and placed the bag on her shoulder. Stepping away from the desk, she started to walk away. Gabriella sat down at the desk.

"How was the day?" Gabriella asked. Hilda turned to face her, still trying to come down from her prior fright.

"Fine. The Frogmarsh company meeting should be finishing in an hour. The Aldridge room will need to be tidied before the Clarkson group gets in at 5pm," Hilda responded as she stood awkwardly. Gabriella started typing into the computer, ignoring what Hilda said. Hilda took that as her cue to leave. She headed towards the door across from the desk, stopping briefly to retrieve her headphones and sunglasses out of her bag. Putting on her sunglasses, she turned her headphones on and placed them over her ears. She grabbed her phone and started listening to some soundtrack music from the film, "A Little Chaos". She felt herself calm down slightly as she walked through the door and out of the building. The summer day was full of sunshine with barely a cloud in the sky. A cacophony of families with children broke any peace with sharp noises. Thankfully for Hilda, the irritation from the sound of screaming children was soothed by the wonderful sound of the orchestral harmony making its way into her ears. She ventured from the building door and confidently walked away.

It's 3:35pm. Hilda was walking up a steep street, still listening to music. The street was full of bright local shops and a small supermarket that also shone brightly in the summer sky. Continuing past the shops on this main street, she turned left onto a residential street. She felt a slight breathlessness which dissipated as the road became flat. She ventured along until she reached a house with a white door. Recognising the house, she walked along the path and reached into her bag to get her house keys. She found her keys and placed the key into the door. As it unlocked, Hilda stepped into the hallway and wiped her feet on the mat meticulously: four wipes on each foot. She locked the door behind her. She grabbed her phone and stopped the music from playing. She took off her sunglasses and headphones, turning them off and placing them back in her bag before she even stepped off the mat. She slid her heeled shoes off and breathed a sigh of relief as she undid her ponytail. Sunshine beamed through the windows, shining upon the walls. She looked around at the hallway full of pictures of a family of three women. Hilda quickly turned away and went towards the kitchen. She was about to grab a glass when she heard the door start to unlock. This perturbed her: her Mum wasn't expected to come home at this time. She slowly left the kitchen and started approaching the front door with anticipation. As she was about halfway across the hallway, the door opened. Her Mum came through nonchalantly. She turned to face Hilda, who looked at her with an expression of slight irritation.

"Mum!" Hilda sputtered.

"Hi darling," her Mum greeted her daughter. She looked at her with a slight bit of concern, "Are you okay?"

"You're early," Hilda said bluntly.

"Oh, sorry love," her Mum apologised, "I forgot to let you know: your Auntie Deborah had to cancel. Your cousin's got appendicitis. That's why I'm early."

"Oh. Okay. Sorry, I had a bit of stress at work," Hilda responded. Her Mum approached her.

"Do you want to talk about it, or have a hug?" her Mum offered. Hilda shook her head, flashing a quick smile.

"Thanks, Mum," Hilda said, "I'll just head to my room." She went past her Mum and ran up the stairs. She entered her bedroom and took off her satchel bag, then sat on her wooden double bed. The purple walls had a couple of posters adorning them. Hilda turned to the window where she spotted her reed diffuser. She went into her bedside drawer and got out a bottle of lavender oil and some reeds. As she placed the oil and reeds in her diffuser, the scent of lavender started to ease her from the stress she felt. Her muscles began to untense, her brain started to unwind, and she started to feel more relaxed. After she finished putting together the reed diffuser, Hilda lay on her bed. She held her octopus plush that turns inside out to show whether one is happy or sad. Hilda started flipping it between sad and happy until she decided she was feeling happier. She placed it on her bedside table next to her alarm clock. She went to her satchel bag and pulled out her phone, notebook, and pen. As she sat back on the bed, she went to Spotify and started listening to a playlist of Leonard Cohen songs. For a while, she was content to just stare at the ceiling, contemplating her thoughts whilst fidgeting with her notebook and pen. Songs came and went in her ears as she gathered her thoughts. After a while, Hilda came up with an idea. She sat upright, opened her notebook, and began to write. She was oddly at peace as she jotted down her idea. Nothing around her mattered anymore; just the very idea in that moment in time. She imagined a world of witchcraft, vampires, and werewolves on a modern day backdrop. Would the mythical creatures be on the side of good or bad? Or is it a more complicated situation than that? These were the sorts of questions she was contemplating as she continued on her train of thought. When she stopped writing, she started tapping her pen on her notebook, almost as if she thought that would trigger a thought that would help her out. She stopped tapping. She looked at her notes again and tried to continue writing, but nothing was coming out of her mind anymore. She sighed as she placed her notebook to the side. At that, a knock on her door was heard. Hilda reached for her phone and turned off the music. She approached the door, where her Mum stood on the other side.

"Hi, love," her Mum started, "What do you fancy for dinner? I can make us spaghetti bolognese."

"That would be nice," Hilda smiled. "Thanks, Mum. It's a bit early to have dinner yet, isn't it?"

"It's 5:30 pm and it'll take me a little while to cook," her Mum kindly explained. Hilda sighed, a little dismayed at herself. She enjoyed her writing session but felt a pang of guilt for her lack of time-keeping skills.

"Oh," Hilda replied, "I must've lost track of time. Sorry."

"That's okay, love," her Mum reassured her, "I'll come get you when dinner is ready." With that, her Mum went back downstairs.

Fifty minutes elapsed. Hilda and her mother were eating together at the dinner table in the dining room. The sunshine had dimmed a little but still shone outside. Despite the table being big enough to fit six people, the two occupants chose to sit on chairs next to each other. They were tucking into their homemade spaghetti bolognese topped with parmesan. Silence befell the two with the exception of the quiet sounds of them eating. When Hilda's Mum stopped eating and faced her daughter, Hilda noticed.

"What is it, Mum?" Hilda asked.

"I had a call today from Kate," her Mum started. Hilda stopped. She swallowed what was in her mouth and looked back at her Mum. A twinge of anger kicked in.

"Is she going to bother seeing us this year?" Hilda snarkily asked.

"Hilda! She's your sister," her Mum exclaimed.

"She would be more of a sister if I actually *saw* her," Hilda retorted. She angrily scooped a forkful of food with her fork and spoon. She continued to eat. Her Mum hesitated.

"That being said," her Mum sighed, "She's coming back to Brighton for a couple of months before she's off on her next job. So you'll be able to see her for a bit when you're not at work." Hilda continued eating, not wanting to acknowledge what was said. Her Mum played with her food for a moment before continuing to eat herself. The rest of the meal progressed in awkward silence until Hilda had finished. She stood up to leave with her plate and cutlery.

"Hilda, don't you want dessert?" her Mum asked. Hilda shook her head.

"Maybe later, Mum," Hilda replied. She went to the kitchen and rinsed her plate before placing it on the sideboard to be washed. She looked at her Mum, who was still eating. Hilda could tell her Mum was a little sad, but she didn't want to confront her feelings over it. She decided to head straight up to her bedroom without another word. As she shut the door, she went to her phone. She went to her contacts and rang one of them. Placing the phone to her ear, she waited for an answer. Instead, she got the voicemail machine. Suddenly feeling nervous, she hung up. She realised what she had done and decided to quickly ring him back.

"He's going to think I'm desperate," Hilda thought to herself. She sighed as the automated message played out. She waited for the beep before commencing her message:

"Hi, Jack, it's me," Hilda began, "Sorry, I must've caught you at a bad time. I'll speak to you later." With that, she hung up. She tapped the phone anxiously. She threw it on the bed, her heart racing. She quickly went back to her bed to pick up her phone. As she sat on her bed, her phone started ringing. It was indeed her friend, Jack. She answered the phone.

"Hey," Hilda answered, "Sorry, I didn't mean to interrupt you."

"It's okay," Jack replied, "I was just in the loo when you caught me."

"Charming," Hilda commented sarcastically. This helped calm her down a little.

"Are you okay? You don't usually call." Hilda hesitated at Jack's question. She contemplated spilling her guts over her chat with her Mum, but something in her heart stopped her.

"It's nothing," Hilda backtracked, "It's stupid."

"Are you sure? You can tell me, you know," Jack reassured her.

"Apparently Kate is going to be back in the city for a bit," Hilda complained. "I think Mum wants me to see her."

"How do you feel about that?" Jack asked kindly. Hilda baulked. She desperately wanted to be honest with Jack, but she didn't feel she could be. A palpable silence emerged between the pair.

"Do you want a distraction?" Jack suggested. Hilda breathed a sigh of relief.

"Is it a friendly distraction, a sexy one, or both?" Hilda coyly enquired with a little smile on her face.

"We can go with both if you're free this Saturday," Jack hinted. Hilda's smile grew.

"Sure. I can be at yours at 10am?"

"Yeah. Let's go with that. I'll see you then."

"That sounds wonderful."

Chapter Two

A portent of doom spread across the city of Brighthelmston as the dark skies deepened. The city's nightlife hummed obliviously with activity as club goers started to congregate. A melting pot of humanity went about their nights with a mix of mythical demons. Cracks were prevalent along the pavements from heavy footed demons walking on them with reckless abandon. Among the vibrant clubs and bars were run down old buildings where vampires hung out in their droves, eating their victims in relative peace. The only true sense of light came from the overhead street lamps flickering away, struggling to keep the streets illuminated. Amongst it all was a woman wandering the streets alone. Her black hair flowed seamlessly into the night sky whilst her eyes were a captivating emerald green. She continued to walk down the road when she suddenly stopped. She could sense someone following her. She turned to see a pair of people behind her, abruptly caught out. She sighed.

"Leaf," the first person started, "You shouldn't be out on your own right now."

Leaf sighed.

"I'll be fine, Argus," Leaf retorted, "Be more worried about yourself."

"We're just worried," the second person continued.

"I know, Vikram," Leaf said, "Neither of you are particularly subtle."

"I mean -" Vikram started.

"I felt you follow me," Leaf interrupted. "I'm a pretty intuitive witch. Besides, who else would follow me around like this? It's not like I have a family who'd get concerned." Leaf stopped at the weight of what she had just said. Her heart panged with grief in that moment, aching at a loss she could hardly stand to face. A tear fell down Leaf's face. Vikram and Argus came closer to Leaf. They stood either side of her and placed their arms around her. She initially resisted but gave into the comfort she craved from the embrace.

"Thank you," Leaf croaked as she tried not to cry. Vikram and Argus stepped back from her. Leaf wiped her singular tear away from her face. She looked at Vikram and Argus.

"I'm sorry," Leaf apologised, "I still miss her."

"It's okay, Leaf," Argus assured her, "I know this is really hard on you, but we're always here for you."

"Yeah," Vikram jumped in, "We're not going anywhere."

"I beg to differ," a cloaked figure gloated. Vikram, Argus, and Leaf turned to face the mysterious figure. They were accompanied by two other cloaked figures. The cloaks were black and adorned with a red trim. The three cloaked figures let down their hoods to reveal their vampiric faces. Argus and Vikram stood in front of Leaf, holding stakes.

"You won't win," the first vampire gloated, "Rex will reign supreme!"

"Rex! Rex! Rex!" the three vampires chanted in unison. At that, they lunged at Vikram, Argus, and Leaf. They each took on a vampire. Argus and Vikram fought against their creatures of the night. Leaf faced hers. The vampire took one step and then stayed in place. Leaf smirked at him.

"Did you really think I'd be *that* easy to kill?" she gloated. She held her hand out in front of herself. Her eyes started to glow slightly.

"Incendere!" she whispered. A ball of fire shot out from Leaf's hand and collided onto the vampire she was facing. The ball quickly engulfed the vampire, who screamed as he disintegrated to dust. Leaf was about to go help Argus when the vampire who was fighting Vikram grabbed her. She struggled, trying to get away.

"It'll only hurt a bit," the vampire teased. He was about to bite Leaf when, out of nowhere, Vikram stabbed him through the neck with his stake. The vampire choked as he let Leaf go. Leaf turned to face the vampire who tried to kill her. Before she knew it, Vikram took the stake from the vampire's neck and placed it directly through his heart from behind. The vampire turned to dust. Leaf breathed a sigh of relief.

"Thanks," she said to Vikram. Leaf and Vikram turned to Argus, who was just dispatching the vampire who had attacked him. Argus faced his friends as the vampire turned to dust.

"We need to go home," Argus demanded. "It's not safe out here for us tonight."

Chapter Three

Hilda's alarm clock blared so loudly at 8:30am that it could wake even the deepest of sleepers. She slammed her hand on it to stop its piercing noise. She struggled out of bed, still half-asleep, and stumbled out of her bedroom. Heading into the bathroom, she yawned and grabbed her toothbrush. The smell and taste of the mint hit her nose and tongue respectively, which helped her rouse from her half-asleep state. She finished brushing her teeth and got out an unscented deodorant from her mirrored cabinet. She was about to put it on when she spotted another deodorant that had a more flowery scent to it, so, on impulse, she placed the other one back and put the flowery deodorant on under her armpits. Once she was done, she went back to her room, this time far more awake than she had been a few moments before. She grabbed her phone from her bedside table and saw a text from Jack that made her smile: "Good morning, looking forward to later." She looked at her calendar on her computer desk. She smiled again when it clicked what day it was: it was Saturday, which meant she was going to see Jack. She went to her wardrobe and opened it to find an array of clothes both hanging from the rail and folded in the smaller compartments. She pondered on what to wear for a while. She grabbed a dress that was folded up. It was a yellow lace dress that went three quarters of the way down her legs. She placed it over herself and looked down.

"Hmm," Hilda thought to herself, "This might be too fancy." She threw the dress on her bed. Instead she reached for one that was hanging in her wardrobe – it was a rainbow-striped strap dress that had a beautiful flow to it at the end. She looked at it for a moment but decided against wearing it. She threw it on the bed alongside her yellow dress.

"Maybe I shouldn't wear a dress," Hilda thought. "Maybe that's too much for seeing Jack." She got out one of her t-shirts. It had a picture of Jane Austen wearing rainbow sunglasses with a saying, "More Pride, Less Prejudice." Hilda smiled at it but quickly threw it on her bed.

"He's seen that one before," Hilda dismissed. "Bloody hell, why is it so hard to find an outfit to wear? It's Jack, not the King of England." She stood in her pyjamas, stuck in a form of choice paralysis. She looked back at the two dresses and shirt she'd discarded to her bed. Sighing, she picked up the rainbow dress.

"I'm going to be late if I don't make a choice." Hilda deduced, "I doubt Jack will be impressed if I'm late." She took off her pyjamas, grabbed a pair of knickers and a bra from her underwear drawer, and put them on. She then picked up the rainbow dress. When it was on, she twirled to see the skirt twirl with her. Satisfied with her choice, she put the other dress and t-shirt back in the wardrobe. She looked at her alarm clock: it was 8:50am. She left her bedroom and ran down the stairs. She went into the living room only to find her Mum there watching the news channel.

"Anything interesting, Mum?" Hilda asked.

"Apparently the 1922 committee is meeting to potentially replace the current wanker with another one," her Mum answered whilst focussing on the screen.

"Sounds like business as usual then," Hilda replied. Her Mum turned to face her, smiling at her.

"You look very pretty today. That's not like you normally," her Mum remarked before she realised what she'd said. "I don't mean you're not pretty; it's just you don't usually dress up. Are you going anywhere nice today?" her Mum commented.

"Oh nowhere in particular," Hilda blushed, "Just seeing Jack today."

"Just make sure you're not home too late. I don't like the idea of you walking home alone," her Mum said in an anxious tone.

"It's fine, Mum. I'm sure if it gets late I can sort something out," Hilda reassured her.

Forty-five minutes passed. Hilda stepped out of her home wearing her headphones, sunglasses, and satchel bag. She closed the door behind her and started about her journey to Jack's flat. She turned on some jaunty Blackbeard's Tea Party music on her phone. Hilda took note of the people going about their regular days as she walked towards the bus stop. She was distracted by the passing fluffy poodle with its owner. She contemplated approaching the owner to ask about their dog until she saw the bus she needed pulling up at the bus stop a few feet down the road. She suddenly started to run in the shoes she chose that were not built for running. She tripped as she reached the bus stop, scraping her right knee in the process. She didn't want to be stopped by a knee scrape, so she got to the bus as it let its last passenger on. She scrambled to get her bus pass out of her purse. She clumsily dropped her pass on the ground but quickly picked it up again. Flustered, she placed the pass on the bus sensor.

"You alright there, love?" the bus driver enquired, but Hilda didn't really hear him properly at first. She removed her headphones from her ears as she processed what had been said to her.

"Yeah, thanks," Hilda replied hurriedly, not directing her look at the bus driver. Before the driver could ask any follow up questions, Hilda put her headphones back on her head. As the bus doors shut, Hilda took a seat next to a window. The bus moved along on its journey along the coast. Hilda looked out the window. She enjoyed the view but kept track of the stops along the way, paranoid she'd miss the bus stop. She fidgeted with the skirt part of her dress. As the bus got closer to her destination, she began to feel as nervous as she'd felt on the phone with Jack a few days prior. This was an odd feeling for Hilda. Maybe it was just the adrenaline from tripping over playing tricks with her mind, she thought, or maybe she felt a bit overdressed. Or maybe, she worried, it was something else entirely relating to her visit to Jack's place. She didn't have time to think about that as she was at the stop before her destination. When the bus left that stop, she pressed the stop button. She got up from her seat, walked to the front of the bus near the driver's compartment, and waited. In the distance, there was a dark haired man waiting at the bus stop. He looked down at his watch before spotting the incoming bus. Hilda's heart raced a little, but she composed herself. She got off the bus as it stopped, straight next to the dark haired man. He smiled at her.

"Hey," the man greeted her. Hilda would know his smooth voice from anywhere. She looked up into his hazelnut eyes that gazed right back at her.

"Hey, Jack," Hilda said as she faced him. Jack noticed the graze on her knee.

"What did you do to your knee?" he asked out of concern. Hilda looked down at it and looked back at Jack.

"It's nothing," Hilda dismissed, "I just tripped."

"Where did you trip up?"

"By my bus stop. I thought I was going to be late if I didn't catch it."

"We're going to clean that up when we get to my flat," Jack declared as they started to walk away from the bus stop together. Hilda felt a bit self-conscious as they walked.

"You look lovely by the way," Jack told her. Hilda looked at him, smiled, then fixed her gaze back in front of her, the self consciousness melting away.

"Thanks."

Three hours later, Jack and Hilda were getting dressed in his bedroom. They were both rather relaxed as they got their clothes on. Jack turned to face Hilda whilst she had her back to him. He smiled at her. She started to turn back to him. He stopped looking at her and continued to put his clothes back on.

"What were you thinking of doing for lunch?" Hilda asked innocently. Jack turned to face her once more.

"What do you fancy?" he asked her in response.

"I don't know," she answered, "I was hoping you had something in mind."

Jack giggled.

"Now you know I'm terrible at making decisions, Hilda. I'm about as decisive as a hummingbird," Jack remarked.

"With both our neurodivergent superpowers, we can take over the world!" Hilda playfully retorted. They smiled at each other and laughed a little. They were now fully dressed.

"We're impossible sometimes, aren't we?" Jack said wistfully.

"I know, right?" Hilda jested. There was a moment of pause between the two when they just looked at each other, not quite knowing how to proceed.

"Do you have brown ale and sourdough bread?" Hilda asked suddenly. Jack looked at her a little puzzled.

"That's random even by your standards. Why ask?" Jack wondered.

"I'm hungry and I suddenly fancy having a bit of Welsh rarebit," Hilda announced, "Does that sound good?"

"Okay, now that makes sense," Jack said as he smiled. "Let's do it." Hilda smiled back at him. She headed to the kitchen with him following right behind her. She stopped at the cupboards.

"I don't remember where anything is," Hilda admitted. "If I tell you the ingredients, will you get them for me?"

"Sure," Jack responded, "What do you need?"

Hilda thought for a moment.

"Brown ale, sourdough bread, butter, flour, cheddar cheese, mustard powder, and worcestershire sauce," Hilda said. "I also need your weighing scales, a cheese grater, a measuring jug, a wooden spoon, and a saucepan." Jack gathered the ingredients and crockery as requested. Hilda started heating a hob on the stove and the grill in preparation.

"Great, thanks," Hilda said. They prepared the ingredients to Hilda's instruction. As she focussed on cooking, Jack handed the ingredients as and when she needed them.

"There's this great pop up food market that's happening next Saturday. I was wondering if you wanted to go with me?" Jack asked politely. Hilda stopped as she turned to face him.

"I've got a horrible feeling that's the day Kate's coming to see us," Hilda replied sadly. The mention of her sister brought an annoyance in her. She went back to the saucepan. Jack was momentarily unsure how to proceed.

"So, she's actually coming over this time?" Jack asked as Hilda removed the saucepan from the hob.

"We can put the sauce on the sourdough bread now," Hilda remarked, seemingly ignoring what Jack had just asked her. Hilda put the sauce on the sourdough slices and placed them on the grill. She faced Jack again.

"I don't know," Hilda finally answered, "I mean, she apparently sent a photo of her plane tickets to Mum but I wouldn't put it past her to mess her about again after the last time she did that." Hilda watched over the cooking on the grill. Jack placed a hand on her shoulder.

"You can talk to me about this stuff, you know," Jack assured her. "I know you find this hard and that's okay. I'm not going anywhere."

Hilda smiled at him. Every impulse in her told her to kiss him, but she resisted. She turned back to watching the Welsh rarebit in the grill.

Chapter Four

Argus, Vikram, and Leaf made it back to their home in one piece. Argus locked the door behind him. Their home was an effective hideout. The windows had blackout curtains and crosses adorned on them. Where regular people would have a living room there stood a wall-to-wall library of books with a quartet of seats in the middle. The books were on a variety of mythical and magical topics including spell books in Latin, weaponry guides that would stun a gun enthusiast, and volumes on monsters long believed to be relegated to the realm of fairy tales. Some of the books had well-worn spines whilst others accumulated dust from their lack of use. The older books that contained lignin smelt vaguely of vanilla. Argus made a beeline for the books. As he reached for a somewhat worn out book on vampires, Vikram and Leaf sat on two of the wooden chairs that creaked at the slightest weight placed upon them. Leaf picked up a laptop from underneath her chair. She placed it on her lap and turned it on.

"What are you doing?" Vikram asked Argus. Argus turned to face him.

"If we're going to face Rex and his cult, we need all the knowledge possible," Argus replied.

"But we already know about vampires. Stake them, burn them, decapitate them - it's basic stuff," Vikram argued.

"We need to know what they might be up to," Argus countered. "There's no point waiting for them to strike."

"How's the book going to help?" Vikram wondered.

"Argus thinks there's a pattern to all this. Don't you?" Leaf said quietly just as Argus was about to argue with Vikram.

"It's worth seeing if Rex has popped up in the past and if there's any pattern to his behaviour," Argus agreed. He turned to look for a useful book. Leaf handed the laptop to Vikram.

"Why are you giving me this? Argus has the research down," Vikram said to Leaf.

"We need to find their next event. Argus is right; there's no point waiting for them to strike when we can beat them at their own game," Leaf explained. Vikram took the laptop from Leaf. She went to a particular book on the bookshelf and picked it up. It was a book of spells relating to mythical creatures.

"Where are you going, Leaf?" Vikram asked her. Leaf turned to him, irritated.

"Just focus on finding their next event, Vikram," Leaf snapped. Argus turned to face Leaf.

"Leaf, we can't fight effectively if we're not one cohesive whole," Argus warned her. Leaf sighed as she faced Argus.

"I need to find the spell that brings back a vampire's soul. I know it's been done before. I know I can do it. I -" Leaf stopped herself as Vikram and Argus looked at her sadly.

"Regina is not your sister anymore," Vikram told her sternly, "She's a soulless monster."

"She doesn't have to be, Vikram. I can bring her back!" Leaf angrily shouted back. She clutched the book in her hands.

"She's not just a simple follower of Rex's. She's his devoted, subservient Queen."

"She didn't *ask* for this. He manipulated her."

"She knew what he was. Look at where she is now." Mad, Leaf got up in Vikram's face.

"You don't give a damn how I feel, do you?" Leaf screamed at him. Argus closed his book and watched Vikram and Leaf.

"I do, but you're being irrational," Vikram shouted back. "Even if you could pull off bringing back her soul, do you really think Rex would let you live for taking away his favourite pet?" Leaf, without another word to say, bolted out of the room and towards the basement. She held out her hand behind her and the door magically slammed shut, almost coming off its hinges as it closed.

Leaf was sitting in the basement, trying to stay awake as she read the spell book she'd picked up earlier. The basement was a dark, unwelcoming place with a small window displaying the rising sun. The chair she sat on was a comfort in an otherwise Spartan room that had work out equipment scattered around. As she fell asleep, dropping the book, Argus crept down the stairs. He picked up the book and saw it was on a page about vampire soul resurrection. He sighed and looked at Leaf. She awoke suddenly and looked up at Argus.

"I just came to see if you were alright down here," Argus sheepishly said as he gave the book back to Leaf. She stood up and accepted the book from Argus.

"Thanks. Did Vikram find what we needed?" Leaf asked as she yawned.

"Yeah. There's an event coming up in a couple of days. We'll need to come up with a proper game plan if we're going to stand a chance," Argus told her.

"I know," Leaf accepted.

"That means you need to get some sleep. We need our witch to be at her best," Argus gently suggested. Leaf smiled at him.

"Thank you. I'll head up later," she said.

"I know Vikram is a wanker for what he said," Argus said, "But he has a point. If you're going to bring back Regina's soul, we'll need a way to ensure your survival. He won't rest until he's vanquished you."

"I know. We'll figure that out once I've had some sleep."

Argus went back up the stairs. Leaf placed the book on her chair and looked around the room. She walked to a box underneath the steps. On top of the box was a photo of Regina and Leaf in happier times. Seeing the picture was too much for Leaf; tears quickly filled Leaf's eyes. Once she started, she couldn't stop herself from crying. The overflow of grief consumed her broken heart as she howled her soul out.

Chapter Five

The sunrise swept the skies of Brighton as night turned to morning. It was 7:59am. Hilda and Jack were asleep in his bed. Jack started to wake up. He looked over at Hilda, who was fast asleep. He smiled at her as she dozed peacefully. He thought about how beautiful she looked even whilst she was asleep with her hair all over the place.

"If only I could tell her," he thought to himself. He had just reached over to stroke her hair when he was interrupted by Hilda's very loud phone alarm. Hilda, in a half-awake state, turned to her phone and turned the alarm off. Jack retreated his hand before she could notice.

"Good morning, Hilda," Jack said to her sweetly. Hilda faced him.

"Good morning, Jack," Hilda grumbled as she tried to become more conscious. She let out a big yawn but covered her mouth.

"Sorry," she yawned, "Did you sleep okay?"

"Like a log. You?" he asked in return.

"On and off, but you know me." Hilda was now fully awake. She sat up. She felt her messed up hair..

"Oh God. My hair. It's going to be such a pain to brush later," Hilda complained as she touched her hair more. She made a futile attempt to tidy it up with her hands but it only succeeded in making things worse. She groaned as she slid back into the bed.

NEW LEAVES, OLD SCARS

"Why?" she moaned as she hid under the covers. Jack tried to uncover her.

"But I look dreadful," Hilda complained.

"I've seen you like this a thousand times. It doesn't bother me," Jack tried to assure her. Hilda showed part of her face but still kept herself mostly hidden.

"I wouldn't say a thousand," Hilda insisted.

"Fine; I've seen you like this *a lot* of times," Jack corrected himself. She unveiled herself and saw Jack smiling at her. She looked at him suspiciously.

"What?" she asked. A thousand thoughts went through his head as he tried to figure out what to say to her at that very moment. He looked at her with trepidation and anxiety, but ultimately he said:

"Nothing. I'm going to get my medication." With that, he got out of bed and headed for the bathroom. As Jack sorted out his medicine, Hilda started getting herself out of bed.

The clock ticked 3pm. A bashful Hilda unlocked the door of her home. She came through and shut the door quietly behind her. She wiped her feet four times a piece as she always did. She crept across her hallway towards the stairs. As she started to step up the stairs, her Mum appeared suddenly at the top of the stairs.

"Mum!" Hilda exclaimed.

"So. You spent the night at Jack's," her Mum stated. Hilda had a difficult time figuring out her Mum's mood from her tone.

"Yes. I did tell you that," Hilda said. She was suspicious of her Mum's line of questioning. A moment of silence fell between them as they both contemplated their next move.

"You dirty stop out. Are you quite sure you don't fancy him?" her Mum asked. Hilda fidgeted awkwardly, trying to maintain composure against the questioning from her mother.

"He's my friend, Mum. We're just friends," Hilda protested as she tried to get past her Mum, who stopped her.

"C'mon, love; you see him far more than your other friends." Her Mum tried to reason with her.

"Most of my friends don't live here."

"But -"

"Mum," Hilda snapped at her Mum, "I'm not having this discussion with you. We're friends. That's it." Hilda brushed past her Mum and went into her bedroom. She shut the door behind her. Her heart raced. She tried to calm down. She saw her laptop on her computer desk. She rushed to turn it on. She took off her satchel bag and took out her phone. She placed it next to her laptop and sat on the office chair. She logged into her laptop and proceeded to set up Word. She tried to start writing but couldn't find the words. She felt intellectually constipated. She had rarely felt like this before. It was as if she was being blocked from her word flow. She started to panic as the words failed to come to her. She turned to her reed diffuser and took a long smell of the lavender oil. She began to feel calmer. She went back to her computer and tried to write again but struggled. She got five words of a sentence out before becoming stuck again. The frustration was building within her with every passing second. She slammed her fists onto her computer desk so hard she hurt herself.

"Damn!" she shouted as she felt the pain course through her hands. The pain was a soothing experience: her brain could recalibrate and think about something more immediate. She moved her hands towards her face and stared at them, trying to piece together where her head was. She looked at the laptop. Her thoughts were interrupted by a text notification on her phone. It was from Jack. She impulsively picked up the phone and read the text.

"I had a great time with you this weekend," Jack texted, "Let me know when you get home safely." Hilda felt the warmth of his message permeate through her. The feeling quickly turned bittersweet as she felt conflicted by the feelings she wanted to squash. She agonised over what she was going to say back to him.

"Don't be stupid, Hilda Leaf," Hilda admonished herself, "It's a text message. Just grow up and text him back." She sighed, thought for a moment, and started to text him back.

"I had a great time with you this weekend too," Hilda typed. "I'm home now. I'm going to try and do some writing today. No rest for the wicked, I suppose. What are you up to?" She quickly pressed send. A surge of adrenaline went through her body. Ignoring this, she tried to open her music app on her phone but dropped the phone. She took a breath in, picked it up, and put some music on by The Karelia. She placed her phone carefully by her laptop. She looked at the Word document, cracked her fingers, and started trying to write again.

The following day loomed over the city of Brighton. The day started for Hilda in the way it usually does on a weekday: with a 6am wake up time. Her alarm clock sounded across the room, rousing her from her slumber. She climbed out of bed and headed straight for the bathroom. As she grabbed her toothbrush and started to brush, she felt a sense of comfort and boredom. She craved routine but didn't enjoy how dull her work was. She gave her teeth a solid brushing as the mint scent started to hit her nose. She continued mindlessly until she spat the toothpaste down the sink and rinsed the residue away. She opened the bathroom cabinet and picked out an unscented roll-on deodorant. She applied it under her armpits and put it away after use.

She went straight back into her bedroom. As she struggled to put her office clothes on, she thought about the irritating state of corporate office wear for women.

"Why does it have to be tight pencil skirts and blouses?" Hilda thought to herself. She brushed her hair and placed it in a neat ponytail. She grabbed her satchel bag and headphones and put them on. She left her bedroom, went down the stairs, and put her shoes on. Turning her headphones on, she started listening to some music on her instrumentals playlist. She didn't notice her Mum coming down the stairs.

"Hilda!" her Mum called out as she opened the door. Hilda turned to face her Mum, confused. She paused her music.

"What are you doing up this early, Mum? You don't have work today." Hilda asked.

"I've got a few things to do," her Mum said evasively. "Are you finishing work at the usual time today?"

"Yeah. Why?" Hilda asked, immediately suspicious of her mother.

"Can you come straight home after work?" her Mum appealed to Hilda.

"Don't I always?" Hilda challenged.

"Just don't go gallivanting off with Jack or anyone else after work." Her Mum sighed as she headed into the kitchen. Hilda was confused but shortly became distracted by the time on her phone. She didn't have the time to investigate further; she had to get to work. She left the house and closed the door behind her. She put her music back on. Over the 35-40 minute walk to work, she had a gut feeling she knew what her Mum was up to. She felt a feeling of dread grip her. She couldn't reason with herself where it came from, but it caused her to stop in her tracks halfway through her walk. Her face flushed, but she soon regained herself. She shook her head and continued her journey, trying her best to suppress her swirling feelings on what her Mum could be hiding from her this morning. She was calm when she came to her work building. As she unlocked the door, very loud alarms echoed across the building. She quickly turned to the alarm system and punched in the code to get them to stop. Hilda breathed a sigh of relief as the alarms stopped. She went straight for the front desk and placed her satchel bag underneath it. She checked the clipboard of planned meetings for different board rooms. She went about opening up each room on the list by opening the curtains, making sure water and clean glasses were in each room and turning on the lights and computers. By the time 7:30am came by, she was back at her desk with her office computer logged in. She had turned her music off. She placed her headphones in her satchel bag as two businessmen started coming into the building. She sat up straight in her chair as the two men walked by. One turned back to face Hilda.

"Good morning, Miss Leaf," he greeted her, "Is the Chapman room ready for the 8am meeting?"

"Good morning," Hilda returned the greeting, "Yes, it's ready." With that, the businessman left with his associate. Once she was sure they were in the Chapman room, she took out her notebook and pen, ready for whatever may strike in her mind. Throughout her 8 hour shift, she periodically wrote in her notebook ideas for scenes and dialogue whilst maintaining her professional duties. She managed to conceal the notebook from the people who came into the building for their meetings.

"After all, the corporate world is no place for creativity." Hilda reckoned to herself. As the day went by, she got prepared for her departure at 3pm. As 2:55pm came around, she started to get ready to leave.

"This is great," Hilda thought to herself, *"I can leave without Gabriella's attention grabs."* Hilda was about to log out of her com-

puter when a woman in a power suit came angrily darting across the room.

"You're not leaving, are you?" the woman demanded. Hilda looked puzzled.

"I will be leaving in 5 minutes, Mrs. Walton," Hilda stated matter of factly.

"You can't leave. Gabriella called in sick and I haven't been able to find a replacement. Someone needs to close the office," Mrs. Walton barked.

"Do you want me to stay behind?" Hilda asked with a sigh of resignation.

"Drop the attitude, Leaf. It's only until 8pm. You can't possibly have better things to do." Mrs. Walton snidely remarked as she walked away. Hilda felt her anger boil with the unreasonable position she'd been put in. She didn't want to work 13 hours, but walking out was not an option if she wanted to keep her job. She felt herself start to cry out of annoyance that her plans had been scarpered, but she held herself together. She didn't want to give Mrs. Walton the satisfaction. She put her things back by the desk. She grabbed the desk telephone. She was about to start calling her home phone number when a woman dressed in a t-shirt and jeans came to the desk.

"Hello, Hilda."

Chapter Six

Day turned into night. Leaf woke up from her sleep. She knew she had to go upstairs to help Argus and Vikram but didn't want to face Vikram after their argument. After some hesitation, Leaf left the basement to go to the library. Argus was surrounded by books on cults and vampirism. Vikram was doing research on his laptop but looked up to see Leaf appear in front of him. There was an immediate tension between the two.

"Hey," Leaf greeted him.

"Hey," Vikram reciprocated awkwardly. Neither of them knew what to say to each other beyond a greeting. Argus looked up from his book to watch the two.

"I'm sorry, Leaf," Vikram eventually apologised, "I was trying to be pragmatic but I didn't appreciate your point of view." Leaf's tension within herself started to ease.

"Thank you," she quietly accepted. Argus smiled as Vikram and Leaf smiled at each other, putting their disagreement behind them.

"I hate to break up the mood, but I've found something," Argus interjected. Vikram and Leaf faced Argus.

"There are accounts of a vampire referring to himself as Rex - King in Latin - in various towns and villages across Europe. The recurring theme seems to be that he turns up somewhere, consumes the town, and leaves it as a vampire stronghold to take over another village or town. The earliest recording of a Rex Vampire King was in the 1700s," Argus explained.

"It seems like too much of a coincidence to not be him," Vikram concluded.

"There are records of resistance. One particular incident involved a woman in the early 1900s who rallied the remaining folks of her town to fight against him, but -" Argus trailed off, staring intently at Leaf.

"What happened?" Vikram asked innocently.

"Argus, tell us," Leaf commanded. Argus sighed.

"The resistance failed. The revolting townspeople were killed. The woman was tortured in every which way for weeks until she was driven to near insanity. It was only then that she was turned into becoming the thing she never wanted: his vampire Queen," Argus confirmed. Leaf paused to process what had just been said.

"Why isn't she around now? I mean, surely Regina wouldn't have been targeted if she was still around," Leaf spoke as the thought came into her head.

"She isn't mentioned again," Argus informed the pair.

"Who's to say she's the only Queen? It's entirely possible he has multiple Queens out there fortifying his other locations, thinking they're his only Queen?" Vikram speculated.

"I wouldn't put it past him, the bastard," Leaf said in a biting manner. The anger she felt towards Rex grew within her.

"Brighthelmston is definitely a step-up for him and his plans. He's never targeted a city before. If we're going to stop him, we have to be ready," said Argus, trying to focus Leaf's attention on the matter at hand.

"Vikram, did you find the next cult event he's running?" Leaf asked.

"He's got an event in three days outside St Peter's church. If we're going to strike, we need a proper plan," Vikram told the other two.

"I know you two don't like it," Leaf started, "But I want to perform the soul restoration spell."

"Leaf -" Vikram started.

"No, Vikram. This might be a great move if Leaf can pull it off," Argus interrupted, "If nothing else, we can demonstrate that Rex isn't as powerful as he claims to be if we can take away one of his Queens."

"I'd have to be within a reasonable distance without being seen," Leaf pointed out.

"Vampires have a strong sense for the scents of those they know well," Vikram warned, "If she senses you're there -"

"I'm not going alone," Leaf interrupted.

"Neither Argus or I would let you," Vikram smiled at her. Leaf smiled briefly back at him.

"What supplies do you need?" Argus asked Leaf.

"I need to find my clear quartz necklace. I know where everything else is. That should be enough," Leaf answered.

"What about Rex? He's not going to stand idly by after Leaf pulls that off..." Vikram asked the group.

"I doubt the other towns and villages had a super human like you, Vikram. He may be an over 300-year-old vampire but he's all smoke and mirrors," Argus encouraged him.

"So it's agreed; we hit the next event with soul restoration and vampire dusting," Leaf summarised. "We'd better get prepared." Leaf, happy with the plan, left to go into the kitchen. She reached for a box of tea bags.

Suddenly an explosion broke apart the front of the house.

Chapter Seven

Hilda looked up from her desk to face the woman standing in front of her. It was her sister, Kate. Hilda was pretty surprised to see her. She didn't know what to say. There was an awkward tension between the two distant siblings. Kate tilted her head to one side and put her hands on her hips.

"Is that the sort of greeting you give to your big sister?" she asked Hilda. Hilda sighed, still trying to calm down from her encounter with Mrs. Walton.

"Hi, Kate," Hilda greeted her finally, "Sorry, you just caught me at a bad time. Mrs. Walton is making me stay in till closing time."

"But you've been in since 7am, haven't you?" Kate questioned.

"I know. The other girl called in sick and something tells me Mrs. Walton isn't going to try to find cover," Hilda answered in a matter-of-fact way. Hilda went back to her computer.

"Hilda, you can't work a 13-hour shift. That's ludicrous," Kate said with a tinge of irritation. Hilda faced her sister.

"I have to do it. There's no one else to cover," Hilda stated.

"Mum is going to be cross if I don't bring you home," Kate countered. Hilda sighed.

"Either you can explain it to her when you get back to Mum's or I can call her and tell her," Hilda argued, refusing to be swayed.

"You can't let people exploit you like this," Kate tried to convince her sister.

"I don't have the option to just walk off one job and waltz straight into another," Hilda said as she got up from her desk, "I don't know about your world but that's not how it works in mine. Now if you excuse me, I have to clear a room and prepare it for another meeting." Hilda left to go to the Aldridge room. She shut the door behind her. Her muscles remained tense as she tried to calm down. She tried to control her breathing with big, long breaths to bring herself back down to Earth. Her heart rate was rapid but started to slow down as she continued to breathe slowly. After a few minutes, Hilda felt calmer again. She looked at the table. The water bottles were empty and the used glasses were all in a tray. She breathed a sigh of relief knowing her work was made easier than usual thanks to unusually considerate business people. She picked up the tray of glasses, taking them out of the room and into a nearby kitchen. She loaded up the glasses into a dishwasher. She then grabbed some clean glasses from a cupboard and put them on the tray. As she came back into the Aldridge room, she prepared for the next meeting in her usual manner. She made sure everything was meticulous before she left. She got back to her desk to find her sister gone. She felt conflicted within herself for the way she spoke to her sister. She sighed again and resolved to move forward with her day.

It was 8:45pm. Hilda came through the door of her home, dishevelled and tired. She clumsily wiped her feet four times each. She closed the door behind her and leaned against it. She untied her ponytail and placed the hair tie in her pocket. She was about to slink away upstairs when–

"Hilda! Is that you?" her Mum shouted from the kitchen.

"Yeah?" Hilda answered.

"Come into the kitchen, love," her Mum invited. Hilda approached to see her in the kitchen, cooking.

"Your sister will be over any minute now," her Mum told Hilda happily. "We're having homemade chicken chow mein as a family." She turned back to her cooking whilst Hilda fidgeted awkwardly with her shirt.

"Can I change first?" Hilda quietly asked.

"Sure, love. Don't take too long," her Mum answered, not turning back to see her daughter. Hilda quickly turned and raced away to her bedroom. She felt like she was going to cry. The last thing she wanted to deal with at the end of a very long day at work was her Mum acting as if everything was okay within their family unit. Tears started to flow down her face as she tried her best not to cry out. She took off her satchel bag and office wear. She got into her favourite pun t-shirt and flowery trousers. She turned to look at her mirror. She wiped away her tears and started to compose herself.

"It'll be fine," Hilda started telling herself, *"You don't have to say much, she'll leave quickly as usual and you can go back to your life."* After a few moments, she was satisfied she was calm enough to go downstairs. She left her bedroom and came down the stairs. As she entered the dining room and took a seat at the table, she noticed how much cleaner the dining room seemed. There were three placemats at the table with wine glasses and a bottle of wine. As she saw this, her Mum came through with two plates of chicken chow mein in her hands. She placed one on the placemat in front of Hilda and one on the placemat next to her.

"Don't start yet. I want you to wait for Kate," her Mum told her. Hilda rolled her eyes once her back was turned. The food smelt so much better than any takeaway one could order. The fresh vegetables

NEW LEAVES, OLD SCARS

and chicken stir fried in sesame oil combined to make Hilda want to salivate. She contained herself as the third plate was placed on the remaining placemat. Her Mum sat down next to Hilda, grabbing the bottle of wine that was on the table and pouring some in each of the wine glasses.

"Why are we having wine?" Hilda inquired.

"It's a special occasion, Hilda," her Mum answered.

"It's just Kate, Mum, not the King," Hilda argued. They sat together in an unwieldy silence.

"When did she say she'd be here?" Hilda asked.

"She should be here any minute. Don't worry - she'll come," her Mum reassured her. Hilda returned to silence. The clock ticked by as seconds turned to minutes.

"This will be nice, won't it, love?" her Mum said as a few minutes elapsed. Hilda half-smiled at her Mum, choosing not to say anything. The pair continued to wait quietly for Kate. Her Mum checked her phone to see if there were any messages, but there were none. Hilda started fiddling with her hair.

"Hilda, sweetheart, please don't do that. You don't want to get hair in your food," her Mum told her gently. Hilda let go of her hair and kept her hands firmly in her lap. More minutes slipped away into the night. Hilda's stomach started to growl. Hilda looked to her Mum, whose smile was starting to fade.

"Maybe we should put Kate's dinner in the fridge, Mum?" Hilda suggested.

"Absolutely not. She'll be here," her Mum insisted.

"Mum, it's been 10 minutes. You said she'd be here by now. I haven't eaten since lunch time and our dinner is getting cold," Hilda complained. Just as Hilda's Mum was about to respond, a knock was heard on the front door.

"Can you go get that, Hilda? It must be Kate," her Mum asked her present daughter. Hilda got up slowly and walked towards the front door. She opened it to see Kate on the phone.

"Look, I'm at my family's. This will have to wait," Kate barked down the phone as she hung up. She turned to face Hilda. There was a notable awkwardness between the two that hadn't abated since their encounter earlier in the afternoon.

"You're late," Hilda pointed out.

"So are you," Kate retorted.

"I had work."

"So did I." A silence fell between the two. Hilda stepped back to let Kate into the house. Kate made a beeline for her Mum in the dining room. Hilda shut the door and ventured into the dining room herself just as Kate and her Mum were having a hug. Kate sat down on the seat opposite Hilda. Hilda sat facing Kate. Another silence fell in the room. Their Mum looked at both of her daughters.

"Well, no need to wait. Get stuck in, girls." At that, both Kate and Hilda started eating heartily at their meals. Hilda was enjoying herself, almost losing herself in the delicious meal their Mum had cooked.

"This is great. Thanks, Mum," Kate exclaimed.

"Yeah, thanks Mum," Hilda chimed in around her mouthful of food.

"Hilda, don't talk with your mouth full," Kate scolded her sister. Hilda intently swallowed.

"Yes, *Mother*," Hilda snidely returned verbal fire. It felt as if at any moment, one wrong word could cause an explosion between the pair. Her Mum decided to try to break the tension.

"So, Kate, what are you up to these days? We didn't get to properly talk earlier," her Mum asked Kate. She had a smile plastered on her face that Hilda found eerie.

"Well, I'm glad you asked, Mum. I've got some good news: I'm going to get my directorial debut!" Kate announced. Her Mum shrieked with glee. Hilda continued eating, trying to focus on her meal. Kate noticed.

"That's great, love. What's the movie?" her Mum asked enthusiastically. Kate turned her attention away from Hilda.

"All I can say is it's a movie about a princess who works undercover as a spy for her kingdom," Kate explained with a smile on her face. Hilda looked up from her food. She felt a pang of guilt for not saying anything earlier, but still felt a sense of awkwardness around her sister.

"That's fascinating," her Mum said as she turned to face Hilda. "Hilda, do you have anything to say to your sister?" Hilda stopped eating and faced an expectant Kate.

"Well done, Kate," Hilda said as she gulped a mouthful of food. She chased that up with a sip of wine.

"Mum, it's going to be great. We've got some promising names potentially involved in the project. I can't wait!" Kate said gleefully. Hilda finished her food and wine.

"Excuse me, I've had a long day and I've got to be up early again. Goodnight." Hilda stood abruptly from the table. Without another word, she headed for the stairs and went into her bedroom. She shut the door firmly behind her. She felt a degree of tension fade away now that she was absent from the dining room. A flood of emotions washed over her as she tried to remain calm. She turned to her laptop, switching it on. As it powered up, she decided to get into her pyjamas. As she did, she heard a knock on her door. A feeling of dread twisted within Hilda. She approached the door and opened it part way to see her Mum standing there, looking concerned.

"Hilda, love, are you okay?" she asked.

"I'm fine, Mum. I'm tired and I have an early start for work. I just want to go to bed," Hilda explained. Her Mum tried to get through the door but Hilda wouldn't let her.

"Mum, I'm fine. Just let me go to bed," Hilda said in an annoyed tone. Her Mum sighed.

"Okay. As long as you're sure you're okay?" her Mum asked once again.

"I'm fine. Night, Mum," Hilda repeated as she shut the door. She sat at her computer desk and loaded a Word document. She began to type furiously as her mind came alive with ideas. Her mind was distracted within the world of her characters as she typed away, unknowingly working into the night.

Chapter Eight

Leaf was thrown from the force of the explosion, but she recovered quickly. She rushed into the living room which was close to being destroyed. The shelves bowed from the pressure of the blast. Books decades older than her lay in tatters, having been destroyed within seconds. Leaf could barely see where Argus or Vikram were. Her attention shifted when she looked to where the window used to be. She saw a dark-haired woman standing across the street, smirking. She recognised her as Regina, her vampiric sister. Leaf was overcome with anger. She took a step forward into the debris, determined to get her. Regina cooly walked away, still smirking in the distance. Leaf took another step forward until she heard a male groan. She turned to see Argus, who was bleeding profusely from his side. Leaf rushed over to him. She pushed on his wound to try and stem the bleed.

"Shit, Argus. What the hell happened?" Leaf asked him. He struggled to collect himself as the agony started to consume him.

"I don't know," Argus groaned, "Where's Vikram?"

"I'm here." Vikram slowly got up from the floor, mostly unscathed with the exception of a few wounds across his body. He turned to see Argus struggling to hang on.

"Call an ambulance!" Leaf shouted at him. Vikram left the room quickly. She turned to where the window was again to see a crowd starting to form.

"Seriously, one of you had better call an ambulance, because if you just came to gawk, you can sod off!" Leaf screamed at the crowd. A distant siren could be heard approaching. Argus started to slip into unconsciousness. Leaf noticed and pressed harder on his wound.

"Don't die on me," Leaf pleaded with tears welling in her eyes, "Not you, too, Argus. Please."

It was the next day. Leaf emerged from the police station, agitated. She hadn't slept all night. She started to walk in the direction of the hospital when she was stopped from behind.

"Leaf," the person called out to her. Leaf turned to see Vikram, sporting a number of cuts on his face from the bomb blast.

"Vikram. You're okay?" Leaf asked in a hopeful voice.

"Yeah. No internal injuries or anything. Here's to being super strong and all that," Vikram confirmed. Leaf and Vikram started walking along the pavement together.

"What about Argus?" Leaf sadly asked.

"I don't know, Leaf. It's hard to tell. He'll take a while to truly recover – if he ever does recover," Vikram told her. "It's a miracle he wasn't outright killed."

Leaf sighed.

"Regina was responsible. I saw her when I came back into the room post-explosion," Leaf told Vikram. She kept her head down in shame.

"We knew this was a possibility after she was turned. It's not your fault," Vikram tried to assure her.

"But I could've done something sooner if I had thought quicker," Leaf lamented.

"You were grieving your sister. You can't surely expect to be at the top of your game at that moment," Vikram argued.

"But -"

"No more buts," Vikram interrupted as he stopped Leaf, "You're not at fault. We're grown men; we knew what we were getting into going into this life. Argus and I chose to stick with you regardless of the risk," Vikram smiled at Leaf. Leaf smiled back. It was the first time she felt able to smile since her sister's death.

"Thank you," Leaf said quietly.

"You're welcome," Vikram reciprocated. "Now we need to think of a plan. Do you still want to restore Regina's soul?" Leaf sat down on a nearby bench. Vikram sat next to her. She thought about it for a moment.

"Yeah. I know what she's doing right now is awful but I just want my sister back in some way," Leaf admitted. "Is that selfish?"

"No. If anything, it might be the better plan," Vikram reassured her. "It's like Argus said: we can demonstrate his lack of power if we can take away a Queen. It may cause him to act irrationally and make him easier to kill."

"I'll need protection during the spell. I won't be able to maintain my own whilst I do this," Leaf explained to Vikram.

"You've got it. No one is going to get you," Vikram pledged to Leaf. Leaf stood up.

"We need to get supplies from the house. I'll also need the Book of Restoration," Leaf said.

"It's a crime scene. We won't get in there without being seen," Vikram warned.

"My supplies are in the safe," Leaf elaborated. "We don't need long: we just need to get in, get the supplies, get the book, put them in a bag, and get out." Vikram stood next to Leaf. They started to make the journey back to the house.

Chapter Nine

Night turned to day. Hilda's alarm clock went off. She woke up with a start – but not in her bed. She had fallen asleep at the computer desk. Her neck was sore from where she had been sleeping. She slowly turned off the alarm clock as she struggled with her neck pain on her right-hand side. She yawned as she looked down.

"At least I wore pyjamas, I suppose," Hilda thought to herself. She stumbled out of her bedroom and into the bathroom. As she brushed her teeth as usual, she struggled against the stiffness in her neck. After she'd finished, she reached into the bathroom cabinet to find some Ibuprofen gel. She placed the gel on her neck and it started to provide relief; Hilda felt it soothe her neck. As she placed the Ibuprofen gel back in the cabinet, she reached for her unscented deodorant, putting some on.

She ventured into her bedroom, now more ready for the day. She changed from her pyjamas into her neat and corporate-friendly attire. She went down the stairs, still putting on her satchel bag. She turned to her right and felt a lessened pain in her neck as she turned. Entering the living room, she saw a note on the coffee table. She took the note to read it.

"You win again," the note read. Hilda was confused until she realised it was in Kate's handwriting. Hilda sighed, irritated. She tossed the note back onto the coffee table. She put her shoes on and headed out the door, locking it behind her. She grabbed her headphones out of her bag and put them on her head. As she turned them on, she got out her phone to listen to some music as she made the 35 minute walk to work. She felt anxious; she kept thinking about the note Kate had left behind: *What did she mean by it? Is there some sort of competition she feels we're in?* Hilda could barely understand, and thinking about it was creating more anxiety in her. As she approached the office, she resolved not to think of it again. She unlocked the office and set about her day.

It was now 3:40pm. Hilda was walking back home from work, having almost forgotten about the events of the morning. She was happily listening to some music by Seth Lakeman. She had a spring in her step as she got towards her house. She went in and wiped her feet four times each. She was about to head up the stairs when she suddenly heard:

"Hilda! Can you come in here?" Hilda stopped at the bottom of the staircase. She turned to see her Mum at the doorway of the living room. Hilda turned off her music and headphones.

"What is it, Mum?" Hilda asked innocently.

"Just come in here, love," her Mum requested. Hilda hesitated, but ultimately went with her. Kate was standing by the coffee table. Hilda's anxiety spiked as she saw her sister. She turned to face her Mum, anticipating some kind of ambush.

"Now I'm getting sick to death of this nonsense between the two of you," her Mum started. "Seeing as I can't force either of you to go to therapy anymore, I've decided you two are going to hash this out. You're going to talk and then you're going to put all this silliness behind you." With that, she left the room and shut the door behind her. Kate and Hilda faced each other.

"Do you want to start?" Kate offered. Hilda shrugged.

"I don't know what to say," Hilda admitted. Kate sighed in frustration.

"That's just classic Hilda: always relying on everyone else to do her work for her," Kate grumbled.

"That's not true," Hilda argued, "I do plenty without other people's help."

"Yes, because children who live with their Mothers at 30 are *so* independent," Kate snidely commented.

"Have you tried earning barely above miniMum wage in a crappy corporate job and renting in this city? It's impossible," Hilda defended herself. Her will to remain calm started to ebb away.

"Maybe you should've pushed yourself better in your studies. Maybe then you wouldn't have dropped out and stayed to be coddled by Mum," Kate remarked. Her self-control dissipated. That comment put Hilda over the edge.

"Oh, screw you!" Hilda shouted impulsively, "You think you're so much better than me."

"No I don't."

"Yes, you do. You've always felt you were better than me. Classic neurotypical behaviour. Just because you have a normal brain, a degree, and a fancy job doesn't make you better than me."

"Do you resent the fact I have it better than you?"

"No. I resent the fact you break Mum's heart whenever you say you'll visit then change your mind at the last minute. I resent the fact you're never around. I resent the fact that I spent my childhood trying so damn hard to have a bond with you only for you to throw it back in my face."

Kate tried to walk away but Hilda stepped in front of her. Hilda was too angry to allow her to leave.

"Too real for you? Here's a nugget of truth: you've always disliked me," Hilda declared. "For as long as I can remember, you've always kept me at a distance." Kate turned away from her sister. She turned back angrily.

"You're the reason Dad left us behind!" Kate exclaimed. Hilda felt her heart break, but on the outside she maintained a tough exterior.

"That's not true. He left because he was a cheating jerk," Hilda claimed.

"No. I heard him and Mum argue the night he left," Kate disputed. "He left because you're autistic. I couldn't forgive you for that." Hilda held back tears, not wanting to give her sister the satisfaction of making her cry.

"You're lying to spite me," Hilda said bitterly.

"You wanted the truth? I just gave it to you. Dad left because of you and your special brain," Kate said back to her in a mocking tone. Hilda felt a singular tear trickle down her face.

"You seriously blame me for something I can't control?" Hilda quietly questioned.

"If it weren't for you, I'd still have a Mum and Dad," Kate returned without hesitation. The impact of her words hit both of them as if they were hit by a truck. Hilda couldn't take it anymore. Before anything else could be said, she left the room. She rushed past her Mum, and headed up to her bedroom. She slammed the door behind her. She heard the front door of the house loudly close a few moments later. Tears started to roll down her face. She tried to stop crying but couldn't bring herself to stop. She got out her phone from her satchel bag. She sat against the door and dialled for Jack.

"Hey, Hilda. What's up?" Jack asked, concerned from the start.

"Hey. Are you free to talk?" Hilda croaked. Jack sighed.

"I hate to say it but I have to get ready to leave soon. I've got a date," Jack admitted. The words penetrated Hilda's wounded psyche like stab wounds. Her heart felt like it was going to bleed. She put on a brave face.

"A date? Well, I better not interrupt you. I'll chat another time," Hilda falsely rallied as she hung up the phone. The effect of the revelations she'd heard came swishing into her head. She felt her hands start to shake and her chest tighten. She felt as if the walls were closing in around her. She realised she was having a panic attack. As she began to hyperventilate, she tried to stand up but fell back down again. She felt powerless against the rising panic. She crawled along the floor, slowly reaching for her octopus plush. She flipped it over to reveal a sad face. She cuddled it, trying to distract herself enough to calm down. She rocked gently as she counted down from 10 to 1 repeatedly. As she kept going, she started to calm down. As she soothed herself, her chest loosened and her hands stopped shaking.

The next morning dawned upon the skies of Brighton. Hilda's alarm clock sounded off at 6am. She banged her hand hard on the alarm clock, almost breaking it in the process. She grumpily got out of bed and headed for the bathroom. She aggressively brushed her teeth to the point that she made her gums bleed. As she reached for the unscented deodorant in the bathroom cabinet, she knocked it off the shelf and it fell into the wet sink. She grumbled as she picked it up. She grabbed some toilet roll and cleaned off the water from her deodorant. She applied the deodorant under her armpits, screwed the cap back on, and put it carefully back in the cabinet. She went back into her bedroom and noticed that she had a missed call and a voicemail on her phone from Kate from the previous night. She ignored it. She got dressed, put her phone in her satchel bag, and placed that on herself. She raced down the stairs. She struggled to lace up her shoes; she normally had no difficulty. She eventually got herself together long enough to finish tying her shoe laces. She put on her headphones and started playing music from her phone. Ready to go, she got out of her house and locked the door behind her. She ventured out to work. As she walked along the high street close to her road, she saw sirens go off in the distance. The sirens grew louder as an ambulance approached with its blue lights flashing. Hilda stopped walking, pressed her headphones closer to her ears, and closed her eyes as the noise intensified. The sound was distressing to her: her super sensitive sense of hearing made the siren feel like it was going off loudly from within her own head. The ambulance zoomed past her, continuing its journey. Hilda opened her eyes and moved her hands away from her headphones.

"That's odd." she thought to herself. *"I haven't seen an ambulance go by in a while."* After a moment, she continued on her journey to work. She opened up the office as usual, determined to put the distress of the previous night out of her memory. She checked the clipboard of meetings and saw there were three meetings in three different meeting rooms. She sighed but put her satchel bag down by the front desk. She went into each of the booked meeting rooms, prepared the glass water bottles and placed glasses at each seat. She also made sure each computer in each room was turned on and opened the curtains to allow light to shine through, making each room ready for their meetings. She went back to her desk and spotted another missed call from Kate. She ignored it again. As she sat down on her office chair, she logged into her office computer. She got out her notebook and pen and began to write down notes. As the morning proceeded, she found little moments of joy in writing down her thoughts about her characters. She ensured her usual balance of corporate conformity

in front of Mrs. Walton and the visiting business people. She allowed her creativity to flow when she was alone. She maintained a sense of bottled up calm that was absent the night before. As it hit twelve noon, a group of business people left one of the meeting rooms, passed Hilda, and left the building.

"That must be the Jefferson company meeting. The Chapman room must be ready to clear," Hilda assessed. She put her notebook and pen away in her satchel bag. She stood up. As she was about to leave her desk, two police officers walked into the office building and approached her.

Chapter Ten

Three days came and went. The night of the recruitment event for Rex's cult dawned across the city of Brighthelmston. There was a stage set up against a scaffolding supporting St. Peter's church. A group of people were starting to congregate together. They looked terrified. There were twice as many vampire devotees surrounding the group of people, encircling them. They were dressed in the black cloaks with red trims on them. Their hoods were up.

The stage was lit up. The group's gaze was focussed upon the stage as two cloaked and hooded figures approached it from the side. They both got on the stage together, holding hands. The taller of the two figures let go of the other one's hand. They removed their hoods from over their faces to reveal themselves: it was Rex and Regina. Rex smirked at the crowd. He looked over at his vampire devotees who were caught up in Rex's presence. Regina smiled at him with pride.

"My friends, welcome. As you know we have been successful in quieting resistance to our cause," Rex declared. The vampires cheered as the group of humans flinched.

"But it is not enough to simply quieten your attackers," Rex continued. "You must crush them and destroy their will! Tonight, you won't just feast on these souls in front of you. You will go on a hunt. You will pick out good disciples to build my army. We will take this city and spill the blood of our enemies!" The vampires cheered once more. The group of humans stood around frightened for their lives. As the vampires continued to menace the humans within their circle, Rex continued to speak. Unbeknownst to him, activity was afoot inside the church behind him. Leaf was surrounded by holy crosses and lit candles. A clay pot containing spell ingredients sat in front of Leaf. Vikram was wearing a massive crucifix around his neck, holding a sharp stake in his hand. Leaf was preparing for the Restoration spell using the supplies she got earlier from the partially destroyed hideout.

"It's pretty stupid to hold a meeting in front of a damn church," Vikram mused. "His arrogance has really gotten to him."

"He's showing off, but we'll have the last word," Leaf told him, "I'm ready now. I need you to be as quiet as possible."

Vikram turned to face Leaf.

"Be careful," Vikram told her. Leaf shot a half-smile at him. She quickly faced forward and started to concentrate. She closed her eyes.

"Vejovis, hear my call. I ask you to restore the soul of Regina. Hear me. Restore her soul," Leaf began her spell. The candles flickered as a breeze swept through the inside of the church. Vikram looked on as the breeze circled around Leaf, her candles, and her crosses. Leaf started to levitate slightly off the ground. She was focussed entirely on her spell.

"Hear me, Vejovis, restore. Restore her soul!" Leaf shouted. Her eyes opened and glowed a light yellow colour. The candles started to levitate alongside Leaf. Her breathing started to speed up slightly as the spell started to form. Vikram stared at her in a mix of awe and concern as the spell continued.

"Vejovis! I call upon you. Restore her soul. Bring her from darkness into the light. Vejovis!" Leaf exclaimed loudly as she continued. The ingredients in the clay pot previously in front of her started to fly out of the pot and circle around her, alongside the candles. Her breathing intensified. Vikram looked around, waiting for an ambush to strike them. Suddenly a great light fell on Leaf. She looked up into the light.

"Restituere! Resituere! Animam resiteut!" Leaf screamed out. A white ray of light emanated from Leaf and propelled itself through the ceiling. The white ray of light surged to the stage and, without anyone noticing, hit Regina in the chest. She fell back in shock. Rex turned back to his Brighthelmston Queen. The white ray of light shone in her eyes. The vampire circle did not break and kept focusing on Rex. Rex helped Regina up. The light faded from her eyes, and she turned to face the church where the light that was shining on Leaf had also started to fade away. She turned to face Rex.

"Someone's in the church," Regina grunted. Rex turned to see the end of the light fading away from the church. He turned to face his devotees and hostages.

"This isn't a spectator sport. Someone has tried to injure your Queen! They must be stopped!" Rex roared. He pointed at three vampiric disciples.

"You three, with me, now!" Rex commanded. He stood down from the stage and made his way to the church with the chosen ones. Regina felt a tingle in her chest she hadn't felt since her turn: she felt her soul.

Chapter Eleven

The two police officers approached Hilda. The solemn looks on their faces gave cause for Hilda to become concerned.

"Can I help you?" Hilda asked politely.

"Are you Miss Hilda Leaf?" the first police officer asked.

"Yes, I am," Hilda confirmed. The officers looked at each other and then looked back at Hilda.

"I'm Officer Hughes," the second police officer introduced them. "This is Officer Watts. We need to speak with you. Is there a private room we can speak to you in?"

"I think so," Hilda said. She looked at the clipboard of meetings and found that the Aldridge room was free.

"I'll take you to one of the empty rooms," Hilda told them. She was just leaving her desk when she was ambushed by an angry looking Mrs. Walton.

"What have you done?" Mrs. Walton demanded. Hilda was taken aback.

"I haven't done anything. They just want to talk to me," Hilda defended herself.

"What is it about?" Mrs. Walton huffed expectantly.

"I don't know yet," Hilda gently explained.

"We need to speak to her in private," Officer Watts firmly interjected. Mrs. Walton moved out of the way as the officers and Hilda went into the Aldridge room. Hilda shut the door behind her.

"Sorry, she's always like that," Hilda apologised. The officers sat down opposite Hilda. A silence descended between the trio.

"There's no easy way to say this. Your sister Kate has been in a car accident. I'm afraid to say that she didn't make it out alive," Officer Hughes told Hilda. Time stopped in Hilda's head as the words slowly processed in her mind. She looked at the officers and looked down again. Her eyes started to prickle with incoming tears.

"Is this," Hilda murmured, "Is this a joke?"

"I'm sorry, Hilda, but it's not. Your sister is dead," Officer Watts confirmed. Hilda looked at the floor. Her heart ached as the reality of what was said sank in. Tears started streaming down her face. She was trying not to cry out, but it was a futile effort.

"No. She can't be dead," Hilda blurted out, "I just talked to her last night." The officers looked at Hilda sympathetically. Hilda looked at them again.

"She just can't be dead. It's not possible! We were meant to have more time than this. Time to-" Hilda cried. Her emotions got the better of her as she crumbled into a flood of tears. She felt all control seep away as she continued her outburst. Everything felt all-consuming to her as she collapsed from the chair and fell to the floor. Both of the police officers went to comfort Hilda. A furious knock was heard at the door. Officer Watts went to the door. Mrs. Walton's red face puffed at the officer.

"What is that noise? People are complaining!" Mrs. Walton fumed. The officers looked at each other in amazement at the audacity. Officer Watts turned to face Mrs. Walton, whilst Officer Hughes focussed on a still distraught Hilda.

NEW LEAVES, OLD SCARS 57

"I don't appreciate you interrupting us when we're in the middle of a delicate situation," Officer Watts scolded. "This woman is coming with us. You are not to say a word to stop her." Mrs. Walton turned to face Hilda, who'd only just stopped crying.

"You best be back as normal tomorrow, Miss Leaf." Mrs. Walton sniped as she walked away. Officer Watts turned to face their colleague and Hilda.

"Do you have any stuff I can get for you?" Officer Watts asked. Hilda hesitated as she tried to calibrate her thoughts around the question just asked of her.

"Uh, yeah, my satchel bag is by the front desk. It should have everything in there," Hilda said slowly.

"We can take you home to your Mum," Officer Hughes offered. "Are you ready to go home?" Hilda sighed. Inside, she didn't want to go home, but she knew she had to. She didn't feel she had anywhere else to go.

"Okay," Hilda agreed. Officer Hughes helped her up.

The car journey back to Hilda's home from her work only took 15 minutes, but to Hilda it felt like an eternity. She didn't make a sound as the police officers focussed on getting her home safely. All she could think about was her last conversation with Kate. She felt an intense level of guilt and shame they had left their conflict the way they had. The words played back in her head like a broken record. She kept wondering what would've happened if they'd left things on better ground. Would Kate still be alive? Would everyone have been a happy family: Kate, Hilda and their Mum? The car stopped. They were outside Hilda's home. Officer Hughes got out of the car and opened the door for Hilda. Hilda got out of the car. She slowly approached her home with both of the officers behind her. She fumbled as she dropped her keys. She picked them up and unlocked the front door. She wiped her feet on the mat four times apiece. She didn't see her Mum waiting for her in the living room.

"Mum?" Hilda called out. She quickly became worried that something had happened to her. She rushed into the living room to see her Mum crying on the sofa.

"Mum?" Hilda called out again. Her Mum stopped briefly to look at her surviving daughter with the two police officers. She rose from her spot on the sofa and embraced her daughter tightly. They didn't speak a word to each other as they held onto each other. Officer Hughes and Watts waited for them to separate.

"We will need you to come down to the morgue to identify your daughter, Ms. Leaf," Officer Hughes said as Hilda and her Mum stopped hugging each other. Her Mum sat back on the sofa as the reality of what was going on sunk in.

"I . . . I can't," her Mum resolved, "I can't see her like that."

"I know it's really difficult, but a family member has to formally identify her before a post mortem can be carried out," Officer Hughes continued. A pause fell in the room as Hilda's Mum continued to stare in front of her.

"Can I do it?" Hilda said suddenly. Everyone else faced her, "If a family member is needed and Mum doesn't feel up to it, then I can do it."

"You can, yes," Officer Hughes confirmed.

"Can we go now?" Hilda asked. Her pragmatic approach to the situation shocked the officers who were comforting her less than an hour ago.

"Are you sure about this? It can always wait a little bit," Officer Watts offered.

NEW LEAVES, OLD SCARS

"No," Hilda rejected, "I want to do it now." Hilda headed for the door. The astounded police officers followed her without another word.

Hilda arrived at the Police Mortuary with Officer Hughes and Officer Watts. Hilda had this drive to get everything done as quickly as possible. There was a woman waiting outside the room they were about to head into.

"Hilda, this is Lucy Morgan. She's your Family Liaison Officer. Lucy, this is Hilda, the deceased's sister," Officer Watts introduced.

"We'll leave you in her capable hands," Officer Hughes informed her as the two officers departed, leaving Hilda and Lucy alone.

"Hello, Hilda," Lucy said, "I need to explain a couple of things before we proceed." Hilda nodded, not quite looking Lucy in the eye.

"It's very important that you don't touch the body. The coroner still has a post-mortem to do and touching the body can compromise that," Lucy explained formally. "Do you have any questions?"

Hilda didn't react beyond shaking her head. She started looking at the floor and fidgeting with her office clothes.

"Seeing the body can be a very distressing experience," Lucy continued in a softer tone. "I'll be right with you every step of the way." Hilda looked up at Lucy briefly but looked away again. Lucy proceeded to open the door into the room ahead of Hilda, who followed Lucy in. The room was dark and hollow despite the lights being on. A body lay on a table. The body was covered by a large, unassuming white cloth. A coroner worker stood by the body. Hilda looked intently at the white cloth.

"Are you ready, Hilda?" the coroner worker asked. Hilda nodded but didn't look at anyone else in the room. Her attention was transfixed. Lucy gave a quick nod to the coroner worker, who gently uncovered the face and neck of the body. Hilda looked at Kate's face. She slowly approached her. Kate's face had a few scratches on her but otherwise was flawless. Kate looked as if she were sleeping, but Hilda could tell there was nothing left of the sister she knew. She felt a numbness overtake her inner core.

"Hilda, is this your sister?" Lucy asked quietly. Hilda didn't say a word. She kept staring at her sister's face. It felt real to Hilda that Kate was truly dead.

"Hilda?" Lucy asked again. Hilda turned to face Lucy, then faced her sister's body again. She nodded silently. The coroner worker covered Kate's face again with the white cloth. Hilda reluctantly turned away from Kate's body.

"Can I go home now?" Hilda asked politely. "I think I have to be with my Mum."

"Sure. Let's get you home," Lucy agreed. They left the room and Kate's body behind.

Hilda and Lucy came through the front door of Hilda's home. As Hilda wiped her feet the customary four times on the mat, Lucy went to speak to Hilda's Mum in the living room. She hadn't moved from where she was left over an hour previously.

"Ms. Leaf? I'm Lucy Morgan, your Family Liaison Officer. May I sit next to you?" Lucy asked her gently. She nodded. Hilda came through to the living room and saw her Mum frozen in place.

"Is it okay if I get changed?" Hilda asked politely.

"Of course," Lucy agreed. Hilda went upstairs and rushed into her bedroom. A feeling of dread and utter sadness flooded Hilda's head. She tried her best not to cry. She took off her jacket, trying to focus on the task of changing her clothes. Her hands started to shake as she undid the buttons on her blouse. She kept trying, but it was no use. In frustration she ripped the shirt apart, tearing off buttons as she went. She threw her shirt to the side and went to the chest of drawers, opening it slowly. As she scrambled to find a t-shirt to wear, she found an old childhood photo of her and Kate when they were toddlers. She started to cry as she saw the picture of them together, before their relationship crumbled to pieces. Feeling a sudden urge for a distraction, she put the photo away where she found it, grabbed a t-shirt, and put it on. She turned on her laptop and loaded Microsoft Word. She felt like if she could write, she could escape what was going on, if only temporarily. She tried to find some words in her head to type, but she drew a blank. She couldn't bring herself to write anything. She became even more distressed as the seconds ticked by. She just wanted a reprieve, but her chosen method wasn't coming through for her. In exasperation, she closed the laptop violently. She was about to scream when she heard a knock at her bedroom. She quickly composed herself and opened the door. Lucy was on the other side.

"Are you ready to come join your Mother and I?" Lucy asked politely. Hilda nodded.

Chapter Twelve

Hilda and Lucy came down the stairs into the living room. Hilda's Mum was still in the same position but now with a cup of tea in her hand. Lucy sat next to her whilst Hilda sat in a nearby chair opposite them.

"Before I start, are there any questions you have for me?" Lucy asked.

"Why are you here?" Hilda asked bluntly. "I don't mean in a horrid way. It's just I thought Family Liaison Officers only come in when someone's been murdered."

"Hilda, please," Hilda's Mum softly muttered.

"No, it's okay. It's a valid question to ask. Family Liaison Officers help bereaved families through the police investigation process. They're kind of a conduit between the families and the police," Lucy explained. Hilda nodded. She thought for a moment before she spoke again.

"Do we know what happened?" Hilda asked calmly.

"What we know so far is that the crash happened around 6:15am not far from here. Another car that was heading the wrong side of the road hit her head on at high speed. We're waiting for results to eliminate the possibility that they were drunk or on drugs," Lucy answered. A silence fell between the three of them.

"I have to let you know that the story has made the local press. It may even appear on the local news, but we don't anticipate it going any further than that," Lucy added. The information was particularly overwhelming for Hilda's Mum, who started to cry. Lucy put her arm around her.

"I know some victims want to know everything they can whilst some victims don't want to know," Lucy said as she comforted Hilda's Mum, "I can give you some information to talk to Victim Support. Would you like that?" Hilda's Mum nodded. At that, a knock at the front door was heard. Hilda went to answer the door. A man she'd never met before was at her door.

"Can I help you?" Hilda asked bluntly.

"I know we've never met," the man started. "I am..." the man stopped. He looked to Hilda, who looked at him with puzzlement.

"I was Kate's lodger. I just wanted to let you know that I am happy to help however you need with the flat," the man continued.

"Thank you. I don't think we'll do anything right now, but we'll be in touch. Is it okay if I have your number?" Hilda said pragmatically.

"Of course." The man took out a piece of paper with his mobile number on it and gave it to Hilda. She kept hold of it.

"Thank you. We'll be in touch," Hilda said as she shut the door.

The next day loomed as the alarm on Hilda's alarm clock sounded off loudly. She punched the alarm clock so hard she broke it.

"Bugger," Hilda muttered to herself as she turned away from her clock. She did not want to face the day in any respect. She didn't want to face a day at work, but she especially didn't want to face another day mourning her sister. She decided to get up from her bed and start getting ready for work. She brushed her teeth, put on her deodorant, and got dressed. She picked out another shirt to wear, having destroyed the one she'd worn the previous day. She grabbed her satchel bag, placed her mobile phone in there, and put the bag on her person. She rushed down the stairs to find her Mum still sat in the position she was in last night.

"Mum? Have you gone to bed?" Hilda asked her gently. Her Mum turned to face her daughter but turned back again.

"Aren't you going to work?" her Mum tried to deflect.

"That's not what I asked," Hilda scolded. "Have you gone to bed?" She didn't respond. Hilda grew annoyed.

"That's it, you're going to bed," Hilda decided. She tried to pick up her Mum, but she was violently pushed away. That act shocked both of them. Hilda stepped back as her Mum tried to reach for her.

"I'm sorry, love," her Mum apologised, "I just don't want to get up from this spot."

"Why?" Hilda asked.

"I was sitting here before I found out she died," her Mum explained, "I've only been up twice. If I move again, she's really dead." She started to cry. Hilda sighed. She felt appallingly for her Mum, but she was aware the time was ticking by. She thought about leaving, but she couldn't do that to her.

"Mum, I think Kate would've wanted you to get some sleep. She wouldn't have wanted you to stay up all night staring into space," Hilda tried to encourage her. Her Mum turned to face Hilda.

"You're a good girl, Hilda," her Mum said. Those words cut deep into Hilda as she moved away from her Mum. She certainly didn't feel she lived up to her words.

"I'm going to work. You're going to bed. Deal?" said Hilda. Her Mum got up from where she was and made her way upstairs without another word. Hilda got her shoes on, put on her headphones, and started playing music on her phone. She got out the door quickly.

It was 9:30am. Hilda was at work, sitting upright and waiting for a meeting to arrive. She felt lost. She would usually spend time on her own at the desk writing in her notebook, but she couldn't write anything down. Her notebook and pen were on her desk waiting for her, but she felt blocked. Defeated, she put the notebook and pen away. At that moment, Mrs. Walton came through the office building entrance with a couple of business people. Hilda felt herself fill with dread. She knew Mrs. Walton would be coming in, but she didn't want to deal with her.

"Miss Leaf," Mrs. Walton barked as she got closer to the desk, "What room is the Summers company meeting in?" Hilda, ignoring her hostile tone, looked at the clipboard to check.

"Come on, Leaf, I wanted to know today," Mrs. Walton huffed.

"Sorry Mrs. Walton, I want to be thorough," Hilda retorted politely, "They're in the Chapman room." The two business people left. Mrs. Walton stayed at the desk.

"I surely hope there are no more theatrics out of you today." Mrs. Walton whispered harshly. Something in Hilda's brain snapped. She lost all care for what would happen next.

"Theatrics?" Hilda questioned angrily. Mrs. Walton was taken aback by the fact Hilda stood up for herself.

"Well, you didn't have to wail like you did. You sounded like a child having a tantrum," Mrs. Walton snidely remarked. This made Hilda even angrier in a way she couldn't contain.

"My sister died yesterday. Of course I was upset," Hilda explained furiously, "What did you expect me to be - bouncing for joy?"

"Watch your tone, Leaf. I'm the office manager and you'll show me some respect."

"Respect goes two ways, Mrs. Walton. You don't get to demand it off of me, especially with what you just said to me. Seriously, what the hell is wrong with you, woman?" Hilda stood up, picked up her satchel bag, and logged out of the computer.

"What are you doing, Miss Leaf?" Mrs. Walton snarled.

"What do you think? I'm going," Hilda said fiercely. Hilda started to walk away, but Mrs. Walton grabbed her by the arm.

"You leave and you don't come back here!" Mrs. Walton screamed at her. Hilda pushed her off angrily.

"I don't care!" Hilda screamed back. She proceeded to walk away, determined to never return to that office again.

Hilda walked back home slowly in a haze of anger and shock from the events of the past twenty four hours. As she returned to her home forty-five minutes after leaving work, she felt the anger from her encounter with Mrs. Walton filter away temporarily. As she wiped her shoes on the mat, she looked up to see the array of family photos still up on the wall. Hilda's heart sank as she remembered the events of the previous day. She didn't want to deal with the emotions that were eating away at her. She didn't want to reach out to anyone. She didn't want to appear weak. She went towards the living room, anticipating that her Mum may have moved back there after she left for work, but she was surprised to not see her there. She quickly but quietly went up the stairs. Her Mum's bedroom door was slightly open. She peered through to see her Mum, who appeared to be asleep. Not wanting to wake her up, Hilda closed the door gently. She went back downstairs to the kitchen. She boiled some water in the kettle, preparing to make herself a cup of tea. As she was about to pour the water, she heard a loud ringing. This alarmed Hilda enough that she spilled some water onto the kitchen surface. She took a moment to compose herself as the house phone continued ringing. She went straight for the phone before it could ring again and answered it.

"Hello?" Hilda answered.

"Hi, can I speak with the next of kin for Kate Leaf?" the stranger asked.

"My Mum's asleep at the moment," Hilda replied, "I'm Kate's sister. Can I help you?"

"I'm Doctor Bishop, your sister's GP. I just wanted to say on behalf of the surgery, I'm very sorry for your loss," said Doctor Bishop.

"Thank you," Hilda said quietly.

"Could you please pass on our condolences to your Mother? I'll try to call again later on today," Doctor Bishop said.

"Sure. Thanks, Doctor Bishop," Hilda said as she hung up. Hilda felt something break in her heart. She had been trying to keep everything together, but there was something about that conversation that really tore into her. She couldn't handle it anymore: the heaviness in her heart, the sorrow, the pain, the guilt. It consumed her. She crumbled to the floor and started to cry out. She felt all of her emotions take over as she collapsed. She held onto the floor as if it would anchor her. Her Mum came rushing down the stairs and saw her daughter on the kitchen floor in a state.

"Sweetheart," Hilda's Mum said as she approached. She put her arm around Hilda, who barely noticed her presence. Everything was being drowned out by her tears. Her Mum started to well up, too, seeing her daughter in so much distress.

"We'll get through this together, love," her Mum tried to soothe her. Hilda sat up, trying her best to stop crying.

"This might not have happened if we hadn't fought the way we had. If I hadn't -" Hilda started in a despondent manner.

"You can't think like that. It's not your fault someone else drove into her like that," her Mum tried to reassure her. Hilda started to stare at the floor, unable to speak.

"Look, I'm going to see the doctor later. If I give them a call, maybe they'll have an emergency appointment open for you. Would you be willing to talk to someone?" Her Mum offered. Hilda hesitated. She wanted to seek out comfort, but she wasn't sure how she felt being vulnerable with a stranger. She looked her Mum in the eye and didn't feel she could refuse. She nodded. Hilda's Mum went to the house phone and made a call to her doctor's surgery. As she was on the phone, Hilda got herself up from the floor. She wiped away her tears and returned to the cup of tea she was making.

Chapter Thirteen

It was a couple of hours later. Hilda was sitting at her doctor's surgery. The surgery was a sleek, new building with a clinical sheen to it. It was almost entirely white, with exception to the blue seats, the wooden doors, and the colourful health related posters. Hilda felt uneasy. She was sitting near an elderly woman who wouldn't stop sniffling her nose, a baby who wouldn't stop screaming, and a middle-aged man who wouldn't stop pouting. It unnerved Hilda as she waited for her appointment time to come. The various noises proved to aggravate Hilda's sensory issues. She couldn't turn on her trusted headphones to block out the sounds that were starting to distress her, because she needed to listen out for her name. She shuffled uncomfortably and started to fidget with her office shirt. She felt incredibly out of place, not just because of her Autism, but because of her clothes. She hadn't gotten out of her corporate attire since that morning. Hilda reluctantly stayed put as seconds felt like minutes and minutes felt like hours. As she felt her will start to truly wear away, a woman in scrubs came into the waiting area.

"Hilda Leaf?" the woman called out. Hilda started to stand up, but the pouting middle aged man stood up before her.

"This is stupid, Doctor," the pouting middle aged man shouted, "I should be seen next!"

"No," sniffled the old woman, "It should be me! I've been here for fifteen minutes!"

"What about my baby?!" shrieked the Mum of the screaming baby. Hilda sat back down, fearing she would have to keep waiting in favour of the other patients.

"I'm the emergency doctor this morning and the patient I just called is an emergency patient. Your doctors likely had to deal with something urgent that has delayed them. They will be with you as soon as they can," the doctor tried to assure the complaining patients. "Now, can Hilda Leaf please come with me?" Hilda stood up again and followed the doctor to her room, leaving the cacophony of irritating noises and scowling faces behind in the waiting room. Hilda and the doctor entered a consultation room which was very cold in nature, such as one may expect from a new surgery building. For some, it may have felt unfeeling, but it felt reassuring for Hilda. No garish or bold colours was the way she liked it. The doctor sat down at her desk. Hilda sat on a seat near the desk.

"Hello, Hilda, I'm Doctor McClay," she greeted Hilda, "How can I help you today?" Hilda sighed, unsure where to begin. She didn't look Doctor McClay in the eye. She focussed her gaze on the floor.

"My sister died," Hilda muttered quietly and quickly.

"I beg your pardon?" Doctor McClay kindly asked.

"My sister. She died yesterday," Hilda said in a slower, slightly monosyllabic tone. She looked briefly at Doctor McClay's face but quickly looked down again.

"I'm very sorry to hear that, Hilda," Doctor McClay softly said to Hilda. "Were you two close?" Hilda sadly shook her head.

"I wanted to be, but I ruined it," Hilda admitted.

"How do you think you did that?" Doctor McClay enquired gently.

"I was born autistic. My Dad left because of it and my sister couldn't forgive me for it," Hilda bluntly said, trying to remain detached. She looked to the side.

"We can't control what we're born with. Autism isn't something you asked for: it's something you were given. If your Dad truly did leave you because of it, then that's not your fault. That's him failing as a parent," Doctor McClay argued. Hilda looked a little bit more towards the doctor but still didn't look at her directly.

"I know," Hilda conceded, "Somewhere down the line I know that. I just don't feel it. I feel -" Hilda stopped herself.

"It's okay, Hilda. This is a safe space. You can say what you like here," Doctor McClay reassured her. Hilda turned her face towards the doctor but didn't look her in the eye.

"It feels like my head and my heart are two very different things. In my head I know the truth, but in my heart, I feel another truth," Hilda explained matter of factly. "Sometimes I don't know which one is right."

"Do you have any coping mechanisms you use when you feel like this?" Doctor McClay enquired.

"I love to write. It's my passion, but since my last conversation with Kate, I haven't been able to. It's driving me mad," Hilda answered sadly.

"Having a creative outlet can be really good for you, but you have to be careful not to use it as a means to avoid things," Doctor McClay warned. "Do you find you do this?" Hilda hesitated but felt compelled to tell the truth. She nodded.

"Have you always done this?" Doctor McClay continued. Hilda nodded again. She fidgeted with her shirt again.

"I can see here you've never had any counselling or any kind of psychological interventions before. Would you be open to that?" Doctor

McClay asked. Hilda kept fidgeting with her shirt, but she did look Doctor McClay in the eye briefly.

"Okay," Hilda agreed reluctantly.

"It'll be a while before you get seen, but I think you could really benefit in the long-term from some therapy," Doctor McClay assured her. "In the meantime, I'd like to see you again in a week's time. Would you be happy to come back at 12pm next Thursday to see me?"

Hilda looked at Doctor McClay again and nodded.

It was two days later. The Saturday summer bloomed outside, but inside the Leaf household, nothing was blooming. It was 9am. Hilda was still in her pyjamas lying in bed. She was paralysed with not wanting to get out of bed. She felt it was somewhat pointless to get up and get dressed until she heard a knock on her bedroom door. She opened it. It was her Mum.

"I'm glad you're up, love," her Mum greeted her. "Lucy Morgan is here."

"Okay," Hilda said as she shut the door again. She quickly put on some clothes, not bothering with her usual morning routine of getting ready. She ran down the stairs. She saw Lucy sitting on the chair opposite the sofa. Hilda sat on the sofa with her Mum.

"Thank you for joining us, Hilda," Lucy greeted Hilda as she sat. "How're you feeling today?"

"I'm okay. Well, as okay as one can be," Hilda deflected quickly. Her Mum took her hand.

"I can now tell you more about what happened on Wednesday with your sister," Lucy continued. "As you know, the other driver was driving at high speed when they hit your sister head on. I can let you know that the other driver wasn't intoxicated at the time of the crash." Hilda was perturbed by this answer.

"So what the hell happened?" Hilda asked directly.

"The driver had a hypoglycaemic attack at the wheel and lost consciousness. It happens in diabetics who have very low blood sugar, which he was found to have on the scene." The mood soured in the room.

"So it was his fault," Hilda deduced.

"He had a hypo, Hilda," her Mum tried to reason with her. "He had a medical emergency."

"If he was having a medical emergency, Mum, he should've pulled over," Hilda angrily retorted.

"What if he didn't have enough time?" her Mum argued.

"That's not an excuse," Hilda said back in a harsher tone.

"But -" her um started. Hilda moved her hand away.

"He was going at a high speed when he hit her. He must've been going at high speed before he had his supposed emergency. Either his accident happened quickly, in which case he shouldn't have gone at high speed, or he knew his emergency was coming and didn't act fast enough."

"Hilda, love, you're getting angry," Hilda's Mum warned her daughter.

"Of course I'm getting angry! Join me, why don't you?" Hilda shouted as she stood from the sofa.

"Why don't we just calm down?" Lucy softly suggested. Hilda turned to face Lucy but didn't look her in the eye.

"Hilda, why don't you go get a glass of water?" Lucy proposed. Hilda couldn't take the situation anymore. She left the living room, grabbed her keys, and left the house through the front door. Aggravated, she felt she needed to cool down. She stepped only a couple of steps when she was stopped in her tracks. She saw a familiar pair of shoes in her way. She looked up to see Jack standing in front of her.

Hilda's heart started to flutter as her anger faded away. In its place was an anxiety facing the friend she adored so much. Jack held a bouquet of tulip flowers in one hand.

"You're not wearing any shoes," Jack pointed at her bare feet. Hilda looked down.

"I know," Hilda replied shortly. A pause fell between the pair.

"I'm sorry about Kate," Jack broke the silence. Hilda looked over at Jack but looked back down again.

"How did you find out?" Hilda asked quietly.

"There's an article in the Brighton Gazette," Jack told her, "I'm sorry it took me so long to get to you. I only found out earlier and I didn't want to intrude too quickly." Hilda looked at the flowers.

"Are those for your date?" Hilda asked, pointing at the flowers. Jack felt a little stung at being asked but quickly understood what she meant.

"No. These are for you and your Mum." Jack handed the flowers over to Hilda. She smelled the flowers and half-smiled.

"They're lovely," Hilda said as she smelled the flowers, "They're nice to smell, too. Not too powerful."

"I didn't want to get you anything overpowering. I know you don't like that," Jack smiled at her. Hilda looked at Jack again.

"I would ask you to come in, but we've got the Family Liaison Officer round," Hilda told him matter of factly. She felt sadder that she felt she couldn't let Jack in.

"It's okay. Let me know when you're next free. We don't have to do anything. We can just hang out, whether it's here or at my place," Jack spelled out to Hilda.

"Thanks. I'll see you around," Hilda said as she walked back into her house.

Chapter Fourteen

It was the following Thursday at 12:01pm. Hilda once again sat in the consultation room of Doctor McClay. She was wearing a less formal t-shirt and jeans this time around. She sat awkwardly looking at the clock.

"How long do I have?" Hilda asked politely.

"Each consultation is about 15 minutes, but try not to think about the time too much," Doctor McClay answered. Hilda looked down at the ground and sighed.

"Ever since Kate died, I've been finding myself getting angry pretty quickly," Hilda admitted.

"Angry at the situation?"

"Angry in general. Last Saturday I got angry when the Family Liaison Officer came round. I wasn't just angry at the news about the idiot who killed her. I was angry at my Mum."

"Why?"

"I think maybe she was trying to get me to stay calm, but it sounded, in the moment, like she was trying to excuse him." Hilda felt the anger bubbling slightly within her as she remembered the incident. The doctor noticed.

"Are you feeling that anger again?" Doctor McClay asked her. Hilda looked scared to answer.

"Yes, but I don't like it," Hilda bottled up, trying to appear calmer.

"Why?" Doctor McClay probed. Hilda had to think about her answer. On the one hand, she wanted to keep up a calmer facade, but she also felt if she was going to make any progress, she would have to do something difficult: be more emotionally honest.

"I'm not sure," Hilda admitted.

"Okay, you've said before your parents separated. Do you remember them ever being happy together?" Doctor McClay asked thoughtfully. Hilda had to have a moment to ponder.

"No. They broke up when I was 4. I don't remember much, but -" Hilda hesitated. All that flooded her head were vague memories of a man shouting. Her anxiety began to bubble to the surface. She faced Doctor McClay, who noticed the beginnings of her distress.

"All I remember is him being angry," Hilda blurted out. "I don't really remember anything else."

"Being angry sometimes is okay to feel, Hilda. It's when it spirals out of control or becomes excessive that you need to really worry," Doctor McClay told Hilda. Hilda started fiddling with her t-shirt quietly.

"Autistic people can find they have difficulty with their emotional regulation. Your primary issue, from what you've told me, is that you don't face your emotions properly. It's good to have a balance; however, you can't be petrified of every scary emotion. Emotions are good. They're what makes us human. Embracing your emotional range is much better for you psychologically than bottling them up," Doctor McClay continued. Hilda was taking in what was being said whilst she continued to fidget.

"Does that make sense to you, Hilda?" Doctor McClay asked kindly. Hilda looked towards Doctor McClay but not in her eyes.

"Yeah," Hilda replied, "I think I'm just worried about totally losing myself or getting hurt."

"The risk of getting hurt is the price we pay for love. Nothing ever runs smoothly in life, but to live a life avoiding love or your emotions is an empty one to live," Doctor McClay explained to Hilda, who stopped fidgeting with her t-shirt. Hilda sighed.

"Is there something else you're avoiding?" Doctor McClay sensed.

"Yes, but I'm not sure I'm ready to deal with that now," Hilda admitted.

"Okay, well maybe next time I see you? I'm away on annual leave next week, but I'd be happy to see you in a couple of weeks' time at 12pm again?" Doctor McClay offered.

"Okay. Thank you, Doctor McClay."

Hilda came back home from her doctor's appointment to find her Mum in a state of stress in the dining room with papers in front of her. There was a strange man sitting beside her. Hilda went over to her.

"Mum?" Hilda asked gently. Her Mum faced her.

"Hi, love," Hilda's Mum greeted her.

"What's that?" Hilda pointed at the paperwork. She stared at the strange man sitting next to her Mum, "And who are you?"

"I'm a solicitor from Harris & Rosenberg. I am your sister's solicitor," the man introduced himself. He offered his hand out to Hilda for a handshake but she didn't take it. He withdrew.

"I take it you're Hilda, Kate's sister?" he asked politely.

"Yes. I didn't know Kate had a will," Hilda answered. "Why have you brought it here?"

"Your Mum was named Executor of the Will. She's legally responsible for carrying out Kate's instructions in her will and handling her estate," he explained, "There's more. There's only one beneficiary of the will: that's you, Hilda." Hilda was taken aback. She was shocked and didn't quite believe what she was hearing.

"That's not possible," Hilda argued with him, "We weren't close."

"Either that didn't matter to her or you were closer than you thought," he commented. "Regardless: the will states that everything goes to you." Hilda didn't know how to handle her emotions at the moment. She felt a rush of guilt and shame seep into her soul.

"Excuse me." She removed herself from the dining room. She hurried into her bedroom and shut the door firmly behind her. Her heart rate soared as she digested the news she had heard. She felt her cool exterior dissipate into an unsteady mess. She didn't quite know what to do with herself. She felt shame for the way she'd spoken with her sister on her last night alive, but she also felt gratitude that her sister thought of her in that way. She grabbed her phone from her jeans' pocket. She still had the message from her sister in her voicemail, unplayed. Hilda thought about it; she didn't know whether it was vitriolic or not in nature. She was scared to listen to it, but she was even more scared of how she'd feel afterwards. She decided to embrace what Doctor McClay had said to her: don't avoid feelings. She had to listen to the voicemail.

"Hi, Hilda," Kate's voicemail started, "I don't quite know what to say. I feel awful about what I said to you and how we left things. It's not your fault Dad left. I shouldn't have said that to you. I don't want to force you to talk to me but I want you to know I love you and I want to sort this out. Let's have a chat sometime. Love you. Bye." Hilda crumbled into tears as she listened to her sister's voice, contrite and genuine. A wave of guilt crashed into Hilda's heart. She was in agony over not returning her sister's call, but felt a relief that her sister wasn't mad with her when she died. The complexity of her feelings was overwhelming for her to deal with. In her head, she wanted to stop feeling the emotions she was experiencing, but her instincts told her to feel: Feel everything and feel in its entirety. An hour later, Hilda came down the stairs clutching her mobile phone. She saw her Mum waiting for her at the bottom of the stairs.

"I didn't want to disturb you," her Mum told her. "The solicitor has gone now, so it's just you and me."

Hilda looked at her Mum.

"Okay. What do we have to do for Kate for the rest of the day?" Hilda asked.

"The funeral celebrant is coming round any minute. If you feel up for it, you can join me," her Mum replied.

"Sure." Hilda agreed. Her Mum quickly smiled at her, then turned away. Hilda stopped her.

"Mum, I have a voicemail from Kate. I mean, it's from the night before she died. I think you might want to listen to it," Hilda offered. Her Mum was shocked. It took her a minute to properly appreciate what was said.

"Okay," her Mum agreed. Hilda played the voicemail. Tears rolled down both their faces as they listened to their departed relative. Hilda's Mum held her daughter tight.

"See? I told you she loved you," her Mum said softly as she cried. Hilda held her tight in return.

It was five days later. The day before the funeral loomed large over the Leaf household. Hilda and her Mum were preparing sandwiches together in the kitchen. Hilda started staring into space. Her Mum noticed when her daughter didn't hand her another freshly made sandwich to cut.

"Hilda, love, are you with us?" her Mum softly spoke to her daughter. Hilda snapped out of it and faced her Mum.

"Oh. Sorry. I must've disassociated there," Hilda apologised.

"Don't apologise. We've got a big day ahead of us tomorrow. It's normal to be a bit out of sorts," her Mum reassured her. She gently rubbed her daughter's back to soothe her.

"How many more sandwiches do you reckon we'll need?" Hilda wondered.

"I'm not sure. I'll have to check the numbers of people who said they'd come on Facebook," her Mum said. "I'll have a look on my phone." She wiped her hands on a nearby tea towel then got out her phone from her front trouser pocket.

"Right, so 50 people have said they'll attend, and that's not including the people we asked who aren't on Facebook," her Mum explained.

"Fifty people won't all eat ham and cheese sandwiches. What about vegetarians and vegans?" Hilda pointed out.

"We'll pick up some vegan ham and cheese from the shop," her Mum answered.

"I still think it's weird that the venue would provide us with snacks but not sandwiches or cakes," Hilda mused.

"They were the only place that would fit us in without going into central Brighton. Do we really want to subject everyone to Brighton's parking conditions?" her Mum retorted.

"I guess not," Hilda conceded. Suddenly, a knock was heard on the front door. Hilda and her Mum faced each other.

"Are you expecting anyone, Mum?" Hilda asked, puzzled.

"No. Are you?"

"No. Maybe we forgot to drop something off with the funeral directors?"

"Not likely. I'm pretty sure I gave them everything." The knock was heard again, this time louder and more impatient. Hilda's Mum was about to go get it when Hilda stopped her.

"I'll get it," Hilda offered. She walked to the front door and opened it to see a strange, middle-aged man at her door.

"Hi. You must be Hilda," the man said.

"I am. Who wants to know?" Hilda asked suspiciously.

"It's me. Your Dad."

Chapter Fifteen

Hilda stood silently at the door, processing what was just said to her. Her Dad stood in front of her, half-smiling. Hilda was confused at first.

"I'm sorry. Did you just say you're my Dad?" Hilda asked politely.

"Yes. I'm your Dad. Don't you have a hug for me?" Her Dad stretched out his arms. Hilda resisted. She wanted to slam the door in his face. She thought about it, but something in her pushed her to confront him.

"I haven't seen you since I was 4," Hilda pointed out bluntly. Her Dad put his arms down.

"I know, but I'm here now. Isn't that the important part?" he countered. Hilda didn't like this answer one bit.

"Not really. I mean, where have you been for the past 26 years? It's not like we moved or anything," Hilda demanded to know.

"I should've come earlier, I know, but I'm here now." Hilda's dad tried to tamper her mood.

"Earlier when?" Hilda asked, unswayed by her father's words. He sighed.

"It's been difficult for me to be away from you all these years," he softly tried to convince his daughter. "I've thought about you and Kate every day."

"It's been difficult for *you*?! How do you think it's been for Mum? She's the one who raised us on her own because you didn't want to be around," Hilda spat back at him.

"You have to understand, Hilda: it was a really hard situation for me with your autism." Her dad tried to reason Hilda to his side.

"Oh yeah, because it was so easy for me, you know, the person actually living with autism in a hostile, neurotypical world with only one parent raising me," Hilda strongly asserted. The longer the conversation continued, the angrier she felt inside.

"Darling, I get what you're saying. I'm here now though and I'll come to the funeral tomorrow. Does that count for anything?" Her dad pleaded.

"No. You should've been here for the past 26 years. I'm not suggesting you should've stayed with Mum, but you should've at least been present for Kate and I growing up," Hilda responded fiercely.

"I'm here now, though." Hilda's dad said in a more irritated tone.

"You keep saying that as if saying it a bunch of times will magically change things. It doesn't ease the decades you spent deliberately absent from my life," Hilda attested. Her Dad shrugged in defeat.

"I can see I made a mistake coming here. I'll go now. I'll see you tomorrow at the funeral." Hilda's dad started walking away. He made it a few steps away when:

"Wait!" Hilda called out. She stepped out of the house and a bit closer to her dad. He looked at her, slightly hopeful. Hilda remained stern in her face.

"Kate blamed me for your departure. She overheard you and Mum argue the night you left. You made yourself clear enough for a 6-year-old to understand that I was, in your eyes, the cause of your departure. She told me so the evening before she died. She left a voicemail to apologise later that night. I never got to find out whether she somehow got past it because she died early the next morning," Hilda calmly but firmly informed her father. Tears started forming in his eyes.

"Why are you telling me this?" he asked, somewhat indignant.

"Because you deserve to suffer with the certain knowledge you screwed over both your children and there's nothing you can do to change that," Hilda continued, unmoved by his slowly forming tears. Hilda's dad turned away and walked off. Hilda watched him leave. She turned around to see her Mum in the doorway. Hilda headed back to her Mum, her anxiety running high.

"Was I too harsh, Mum?" Hilda asked, seeking reassurance. Her Mum hugged her.

"I'm really proud of you, love," her Mum whispered as she held her.

The day of the funeral came. It was 11am and an uncharacteristically dark day outside, with clouds looming overhead. Hilda sat on her bed. She was wearing a black dress with a purple scarf neatly placed around her neck. She felt numb in her heart. She was going through the motions as she got herself off of the bed, picked up her satchel bag, and left her bedroom. She went into the bathroom and grabbed a packet of tissues, placing them in her bag. She sighed as she looked in the mirror. She didn't look long before proceeding down the stairs. She went into the living room where her Mum was sitting on the sofa, holding a set of notes in her hand. She turned to face Hilda.

"I don't know if I can do this," her Mum softly told her daughter, "I don't know if I can go through with this." Hilda sat next to her.

"We've got to Mum," Hilda said to her Mum, "We've got to do this for Kate."

"I know. I just don't know if I can read this," her Mum explained, holding up her notes. Hilda took the notes from her.

NEW LEAVES, OLD SCARS

"Do you want me to do it?" Hilda asked. Her Mum shook her head initially but then nodded.

"I don't. I don't want us in this mess but -" her Mum trailed off, "If you get stuck or feel you can't continue, I'll come and do it for you." Hilda nodded. She put the notes in her satchel bag. Hilda got up and put her shoes on. At that moment, a knock was heard on the door. Her heart dropped as she opened the door. Her Mum came up behind her. A gentleman in formal funeral attire stood in front of Hilda and her Mum.

"Good morning. We're ready for you when you are," the gentleman told her. Hilda turned to face her Mum. She then turned back. Hilda came through the door and saw the two black funeral cars. The one car had a door open, inviting Hilda and her Mum to sit inside. The one behind that one was a hearse with a coffin inside adorned with white and yellow flowers that spelt Kate's name. Hilda stopped dead in her tracks. She was frozen as she stared at the hearse. She wanted to run back into the house. She didn't want to deal with what she had to face that day. She felt her Mum's hand on her shoulder.

"C'mon love, we've got to go," she told Hilda kindly. After another second, Hilda broke her gaze. She headed for the open door of the black car and got in with her Mum. As the car started to move slowly through the streets, a collection of neighbours watched them go by. Hilda felt self-conscious being watched by so many strangers. She kept looking at the seat in front of her, staring at the stitching to distract her brain a little. She looked up to find that they were close to the crematorium. She looked to her Mum, who dabbed a tear from her eye with a tissue. Hilda breathed deeply, mentally preparing herself for the ceremony. The car stopped. They were right by the crematorium chapel. All of the other funeral attendants who were inside the chapel turned to face them. Hilda was surprised to see the chapel was packed.

She held her Mum's hand as the funeral attendants prepared to bring out Kate's coffin.

"We've got each other, love," her Mum told her. "Just remember to breathe." Hilda nodded as they began the quiet, sad walk down the aisle. The chapel was full of people sitting in rows. There was a row left for the immediate family that was empty. Hilda and her mother sat there together and placed their bags in front of them. The funeral attendants brought in the coffin to the front of the chapel, and the celebrant began the service. It all blended into a blur for Hilda. It was as if the celebrant's lips were moving, but no sound was coming out. Before she knew it, it was the moment Hilda was asked to come up to give the eulogy for her sister. She got her notes out of her satchel bag, slowly rose, and headed for the podium. All of the eyes of the chapel were laser focussed on her. She looked at her notes but abandoned them.

"I don't want to be here, you don't want to be here, and I'm pretty sure Kate would rather be elsewhere, too," Hilda started. "Growing up, I used to believe that Kate was the cleverest person in the world. She knew so much about everything. We used to get these Encyclopedia books every week and she'd read out bits to me. She'd answer my various irritating questions. We both loved watching tv together. "The Simpsons" was a treasured weekly event in our house. We could quote most of the first 10 seasons without difficulty." Hilda paused as she looked at all the people looking at her. She felt incredibly nervous. She looked towards her Mum who flashed her a quick thumbs up.

"As adults, she travelled a lot for work. She travelled to a lot of places around the world, pursuing her love for filmmaking. We shared a passion for storytelling and bringing fictional worlds to life," Hilda continued. "I aspire to be able to make my dreams come true in the way she was starting to make hers come true. She knew she wanted to be a director and she was on the cusp of making that happen for herself. It's something I wish I could tell her...." Hilda trailed off. She started to tear up but kept it together.

"I wish I could tell her how proud I am of her. I wish I could tell her how much I love her. I wish I could tell her how much I miss her," Hilda concluded. "Kate is survived by her Mum, Matilda, myself, and all of you people here today." Hilda looked out to the crowd who started to sporadically applaud her.

"I don't -" Hilda started to say but she stopped herself as the applause started to die down.

An hour passed. The funeral attendees were now at the Lucky Seagull cafe, eating the sandwiches Hilda and her Mum had prepared the day before. Hilda sat on her own whilst her Mum mingled with a group of attendees. Hilda looked around her at the various strangers that stood near her. She felt incredibly anxious and uneasy to be around so many strange people. She started to feel almost claustrophobic. Just as she felt another panic attack on the horizon, a familiar face came looking for her: it was Jack.

"Hey, sorry I missed the funeral. Damn meeting ran longer than I expected," Jack explained to her, "How're you holding up?" Hilda shook her head, still cooling off from the panic she felt.

"It's so surreal," Hilda told him. "Kate's been dead for more than a fortnight, but it doesn't seem real somehow today. I almost expected her to rise from her coffin shouting, 'Surprise, suckers!'"

"It's still pretty raw. You need some time," Jack advised her.

"It didn't help that my Dad showed up yesterday," Hilda told him. He was stunned.

"Your father? After all these years, he had the nerve to show up?!" Jack said angrily.

"Yeah, but I get the feeling he won't come back after what I said to him," Hilda said confidently.

"That's my Hilda all right," Jack said impulsively and longingly. He realised what he had said and decided to quickly move on before Hilda could process it, "Uh, so, I was wondering. Did you want to come by tomorrow to watch a movie? Or would you prefer I came to yours?" Hilda lit up at the idea of a little slice of normalcy.

"Yeah. I'll check with Mum, but I doubt she'd mind you coming over," Hilda agreed.

"Let's do it then," Jack concluded. They smiled at each other in a way Hilda hadn't smiled in weeks.

Chapter Sixteen

Another week went by in the Leaf household. Hilda and her Mum were sitting together going through paperwork in the dining room. Her Mum sighed.

"Have you thought more about what I said?" Hilda's Mum asked her.

"What do you mean?" Hilda asked in return.

"Kate's old flat. It's going to go empty once Ivan moves out of there next week. It would be a real shame to let that flat go like that," her Mum explained. Hilda thought about it for a moment.

"I don't know. On the one hand, I know you're right. It is mine now, and perhaps it'll be good for me to fly the nest," Hilda considered.

"I sense a 'but' coming," her Mum anticipated.

"But," Hilda continued, giving her a look as she did, "I'm scared to move out on my own. I haven't tried since university."

"I know, love, but this is too good an opportunity to pass up," her Mum argued. "Besides, if you sell it, what exactly are you going to do with the money?" Hilda thought about it. She hadn't properly considered the alternative. She sighed. Her Mum put her hand on her arm.

"You would have a roof over your head with only the bills to pay for. You don't even have to find a job right away with your savings provided you're sensible," her Mum assured her. "I know you're scared, but this is a really good chance for a fully independent life."

"Okay," Hilda agreed. "Once Ivan has moved out, I'll start moving in." Her Mum hugged her.

"I'll miss you, but I'm really proud of you," her Mum said. Hilda half-smiled at her Mum.

"Thanks, Mum," Hilda said as she sat back down in her seat.

"Do you still want to come to the court hearing tomorrow?" her Mum asked. Hilda fidgeted with her hands.

"I think I should. I don't want that scumbag to think he can get away with it," Hilda answered strongly.

"Even if he pleads guilty, he's still looking at at least four years in prison," her Mum reasoned. Hilda stood up from the table. A feeling of tension and unease grew within her.

"I'm not sure I can handle this conversation right now, Mum," Hilda said. "I feel weird."

"Okay, we don't have to talk about him," her Mum backed off from the subject. "Why don't you give Jack a call? You haven't seen him since last week." Hilda felt a little bit of relief in hearing Jack being mentioned.

"Yeah. I'll see if he's free this weekend. I'll text him," Hilda agreed. She sat back down at the table. She got out her phone and started to text Jack. She spent a while considering what she was going to say. She found herself in a conundrum as to how she should ask him whether he wanted to hang out or not. She put her phone down on the table.

"Mum?"

"Yes, Hilda?"

"What do you do when you like someone?"

NEW LEAVES, OLD SCARS

Her Mum paused for a moment. She faced her.

"Do you like Jack?" Her Mum asked hopefully. Hilda felt naked and exposed in the moment. Her heart raced as she hesitated for an answer. Her Mum put her arm around her.

"He's a lovely man and I think you two would work. I just worry you're going through enough as it is right now," Her Mum mused. "After all, you only lost your sister and your job a few weeks ago, and you're about to move into your own home. I worry that if you rush into something, it won't work and it'll ruin your friendship. You don't need more trauma." Hilda understood what her Mum was saying. It made a lot of sense to her.

"Thanks, Mum. I'll wait for a while," Hilda decided. She picked up her phone again, but then she put it down again, feeling a sense of guilt come over for thinking of something other than Kate.

"Am I-?" Hilda started. Her Mum patiently looked at her.

"Am I bad for thinking about something other than Kate?" Hilda asked. Her Mum got up and held her from behind.

"No. Kate wouldn't want you in perpetual mourning," her Mum reassured her as she let her go. Hilda decided to text Jack a very straightforward text asking him if he wanted to come over that weekend. After she was done, she left the phone on the table. After a minute, her phone went off. It was a text back from Jack that simply said: "Yes."

Saturday came. It was a sunny afternoon outside where the sun shone brightly and the seagulls squawked their unmelodious chants for scraps of sustenance. Hilda and Jack sat in her garden together. They were drinking lemonade, wearing sunglasses, and enjoying each other's company.

"I don't know why we've never done this before," Jack wondered.

"Sitting in the garden?" Hilda asked.

"Yeah. Just sitting out in the sun," Jack answered.

"I mean, I am almost as pale as Dracula and I wilt in the sun without a lot of Factor 50 sun cream," Hilda quipped, "but I see what you mean. This is very relaxing."

"Do you ever come out here with a book and read?" Jack queried.

"I have done so from time to time. I usually have the parasol out so I can stay in the shade, but the damn thing broke last year and we haven't gotten around to replacing it," Hilda replied. "I suppose I could replace it for Mum if I knew where to get a good one."

"Why don't we have a look for one on Amazon?" Jack suggested. As he loaded Amazon on his phone, Hilda brought her chair closer to Jack so she could see, too. They leaned in close to each other to look over the phone together. As they browsed, they got even closer to each other. Hilda and Jack turned to face each other at the same time. The romantic tension grew between them as they hesitated. Both wanted to kiss each other. They looked into each other's eyes for a precarious moment between the pair. Just as they were about to crack, a seagull came swooping between them, interrupting their moment. The seagull was shooed away by both Jack and Hilda, who were both relieved and disappointed at the intervention.

"You okay?" Jack asked Hilda.

"Yeah. You?" Hilda asked in return.

"Yeah," Jack assured her. They smiled at each other. They went back to looking at parasols on Amazon, browsing in silence. This harmony continued until a pop up from OkCupid came up on Jack's phone. Hilda withdrew from him, evidently a little stung by the fact he was on a dating site. She quickly concealed her feelings by grabbing her lemonade glass.

"Ooh, here's one. It's colourful, just like you," Jack showed her a parasol on Amazon. Hilda took a look, determined to distract herself from her pain. She saw it: it was a rainbow parasol. She instantly liked it. He clearly knew her well.

"Would my Mum like it though?" Hilda wondered.

"She'll look at it and think of you: of course she'll like it," Jack reassured her.

"At least I can leave a permanent reminder of myself in the garden," Hilda considered.

"I'll order it and you send me the money. Deal?" Jack extended his hand for a mock handshake. Hilda thought for a moment but decided to take his hand. They did an exaggerated handshake together. They separated their hands once again and smiled.

"Make sure to send it to this address," Hilda requested. "I should receive it before I move."

"Move?" Jack panicked for a moment.

"I haven't really discussed Kate's will, have I? She left me pretty much everything. I'm going to move into her flat near the county hospital," Hilda informed him. Jack smiled, his panic fading away from his face.

"You won't be that far from me," Jack surmised happily. Unfortunately for them, an alarm went off on Jack's phone.

"Ah, sorry Hilda, I've got to go," Jack told her. "I've got the engineer coming round to fix the boiler in a bit." Jack got up from his chair, taking his phone in his hand. He turned to face Hilda again.

"I'll see you around?" he said hopefully. Hilda stood and faced him.

"Yeah. See you around," she said in return.

A few hours went by. Hilda was sitting in her room, contemplating what to do. She looked at her laptop. She hadn't had it switched on for weeks, unable to write a single word down on her draft. She considered turning it on again but felt this was pointless. She wasn't feeling as inspired as she did before Kate's death. She felt stuck in a prison in her head, unable to break free from the writer's block. She fidgeted with her t-shirt, trying to conjure up a thought in her head, but it was to no avail. At that moment, a knock was heard at her bedroom door. Hilda looked toward the door.

"Mum?" Hilda called out. She got no response. She thought that was odd.

"Mum?" she said, a little louder this time. No response. She sighed and decided to get up from her bed.

"Okay, I'll come answer the door," Hilda said, a little irritated. She got up from her bed, headed for the door, and opened it, fully expecting to see her Mum. She didn't. She saw Jack standing there. Hilda was taken aback but glad to see him. He seemed a little nervous to see her.

"Hey. I thought you left?" she greeted him.

"Hey. Can we talk?" Jack asked. This created a pit of despair inside Hilda's insides. She knew what those words have meant before and they're never usually good.

"Okay. Come in," Hilda let Jack in. She sat on the bed whilst he sat on the office chair. He fidgeted with his hands and then looked at Hilda.

"I've wanted to have this conversation for a while, but I know you've been going through a lot lately with your sister and your job. I know it's not been very long since that all happened, so maybe this is too soon, but -" Jack stopped himself. He was a bundle of nerves. He knew, in his heart, that he had to tell Hilda something very important. He sighed.

"I had a date," Jack continued.

"I know. You told me just beforehand," Hilda explained matter of factly.

"It went fine. Nothing mind-blowing, but you don't expect that from a first date. I was thinking of going on a second with her but I-" Jack stopped himself again. He stood from the office chair and sat next to Hilda on the bed.

"We've been friends for a long time. I don't want to ruin that," Jack continued. Hilda felt like she knew where this was going. The feeling inside her only got worse.

Chapter Seventeen

"I have feelings for you," Jack admitted. Hilda didn't feel able to say anything productive or coherent. She was shocked by what she had just heard. She was fully prepared to hear him say something completely different. She didn't quite know how to react; she was happy, but she almost didn't want to believe what was being said to her. She turned slowly to face Jack.

"I'm sorry, I think I had a moment: what did you just say?" Hilda asked.

"I have feelings for you. I'm not just talking about friendly ones," Jack started to answer.

"I got that part," Hilda interrupted him. "I just... I'm confused. It's me."

"Yes. It's you I want to be with. I don't just want sex when we're single: I want more than that," Jack told her. Hilda got up from the bed, facing away from Jack. She flashed a smile on her face before turning back to him with a more serious expression.

"Are you sure, though?" Hilda doubted him. "Are you sure you don't just feel bad for me?"

"I wanted to discuss this before Kate died, but now that she's passed away, I wanted to wait before saying anything," Jack countered.

"So why tell me now?" Hilda queried.

"I couldn't resist the impulse anymore," Jack responded. "Classic ADHD impulse control issues." Hilda sat back down on the bed next to Jack.

"I have feelings for you, too," Hilda said, smiling as she made her admission. Jack smiled back at her.

"It's just -" Hilda continued, "I don't know how ready I am for this. I'm still dealing with losing Kate, losing my job, and moving out. I need some more time before I can commit. I'm sorry." Hilda started to dread Jack's response. Her heart started to race as she awaited his reply. Her hands started to shake until they were held by Jack.

"Don't worry, Hilda. I would've been more worried if you'd jumped into things immediately," Jack reassured her. "I know you need more time. You're going through enough as it is. I just hope you're okay with me telling you what I told you."

"I'm more than okay," Hilda smiled at him. They kissed, satisfied in the knowledge that they weren't hiding anything from each other anymore. Jack got up from the bed.

"There is one thing I want to do: are you happy to agree not to see anyone else whilst I wait?" Jack proposed.

"I think that's reasonable," Hilda agreed. "It's not like I'm particularly interested in anyone else anyway, so I've nothing to lose." They smiled at each other.

"Let me know when you get home safely?" Hilda asked sweetly.

"I will," Jack agreed. He left. Suddenly, a surge of inspiration came through Hilda's head. She was elated. She turned on the computer and excitedly waited for Microsoft Word to load. She sat at her office chair and placed her fingers delicately over the keyboard, ready to pounce on the keys. She wrote for a short while, but it was enough to get that sense of contentment she hadn't felt in weeks. It added to the overwhelming joy she felt – a joy she previously felt she didn't deserve to feel. She was going to enjoy it whilst it lasted, she resolved, as she continued to write.

It was 7am the next day. Hilda was woken up suddenly by a loud thud coming from above. She was confused by the noise. She quickly got out of bed and went into the upstairs hallway. The ladder leading to the attic was down. The attic was lit by a singular light. Hilda crept quietly up the ladder into the dimly lit attic to find her Mum surrounded by boxes and old furniture. Her dishevelled Mum looked up at Hilda, who was confused by what she was doing up so early.

"Mum? Are you okay?" Hilda asked.

"I couldn't sleep," her Mum told her. "All I could keep thinking about was Kate." Hilda shuffled uncomfortably and fidgeted with her pyjama top.

"So why are you up here?" Hilda eventually asked.

"I wanted to sort through some of the old furniture to see if you can take them to the flat, but I got distracted by yours and Kate's old drawings and school work," her Mum answered. Hilda felt uneasy, but she sensed her need for nostalgia. She decided to sit across from her to join in. She watched her Mum carefully extract old homework and items from a box that sat between them.

"Oh, I remember this," her Mum said as she spotted an old photo album of Kate's, "This was from her A-level Photography class. She had to photograph the environment so she decided to photograph round Beachy Head." Her Mum handed the album to Hilda. She opened it and looked at the photographs, captivated by them.

"I remember when we went. That place always gave me bad vibes," Hilda shuddered. "But she made it look less creepy and more beautiful." Hilda placed the album carefully to the side as her Mum kept exploring.

"Oh! School photos. This is one of you and Kate when she was 8 and you were 6." Her Mum smiled as she saw the photograph. She showed Hilda, who half-smiled at the photo.

"I recall that day," Hilda remembered. "Adele Hawkins tried to pinch my new Robin Hood lunchbox but Kate stopped her."

"I remember! That headteacher of yours tried to suspend Kate. She soon saw what a mistake that would've been," her Mum joined in. Hilda grabbed a box and started going through it. She found an old story she'd written when she was young.

"Ah, my first creative writing homework. I must've been about 7 or 8," Hilda reminisced. She handed the story to her Mum.

"I knew you'd found your newest hyperfixation when you came home from school that day," her Mum recalled. "Do you remember what it was about?" Hilda shook her head.

"It was about a pair of sisters who fought together to save the world," her Mum informed Hilda. Hilda burst into tears. The memory came flooding back to her. Her Mum stepped carefully around the box to embrace her daughter.

"Sorry, Mum," Hilda apologised, "I wish I was closer to Kate when she was alive." Her Mum soothed her.

"It's okay. You did what you could with what you had," her Mum reassured Hilda. "You both did."

"It's not Kate's fault Dad poisoned her the way he did," Hilda said angrily. Her tears started to fade with her anger. Her Mum rubbed her hand on Hilda's arm.

"Try not to waste your time on that man," her Mum advised. "Trust me: no good will come of it."

"Why does he get to walk around as if he doesn't have a care in the world? How come he gets to breathe and Kate doesn't?" Hilda asked bitterly.

"We can't think like that, love," her Mum asserted. "Life sometimes isn't fair. You know that. The world can seem like an apathetic place. We just have to make our own meaning in our lives." Her Mum squeezed her daughter tight before going back to her previous spot. Now calm, Hilda reached for the box of childhood treasures she'd started to go through before. She found Kate's old DSLR camera.

"We never got this fixed," Hilda exclaimed as she held up the camera.

"They probably don't do the parts anymore," her Mum explained. "Besides, who'd use it? It's been a good 14 or 15 years since she used that." Hilda looked at it again. It looked very much like a regular functioning camera.

"Can I keep this?" Hilda asked.

"Why would you want to keep that, love?" her Mum wondered, perplexed.

"I'm moving into Kate's flat next weekend. It would be nice to keep something of hers there from happier times," Hilda declared. Her Mum was moved by what Hilda had said.

"Sure. It would look great hanging on the wall," her Mum conceded. Hilda took the camera. She left the attic and placed the camera lovingly on her computer desk in her bedroom.

Later on that day, Hilda was sitting at her laptop browsing for jobs to apply for. She didn't particularly want to work in anything other than writing, but she knew full well how difficult it is to pursue a career in writing. She found a receptionist job to apply for within an office setting. She decided to apply via the website but was aggrieved to discovery that they expected a full grammar test to accompany the application.

"Bloody hell, next they'll spring a Maths test on me," Hilda thought to herself. She continued with the test, ensuring she thought about every question as thoughtfully as possible. Once she'd finished the test, she uploaded her CV to accompany her application as instructed. As she did so, she heard a knock on her bedroom door. She got up from her computer desk and opened the door. Her Mum stood in the hallway.

"I have to go into a meeting tomorrow to sort out the start of school with the Assistant Head," her Mum announced. "I know I haven't really left you alone like this since Kate passed away. Will you be okay?"

"I'll be okay, Mum. You need to go to work," Hilda responded bluntly. Her Mum smiled at her.

"I'll likely be out all day. I want you to promise you'll actually eat something," her Mum grilled.

"I eat!" Hilda protested. Her Mum folded her arms.

"Last time you were left in the house alone whilst I was at work, you forgot to eat all day because you were too busy writing," her Mum argued.

"That happened once!" Hilda countered.

"I don't want to nag, but once is bad enough," Her Mum reasoned. "Just promise me you'll eat something whilst I'm out."

"Okay Mum. I promise I'll eat something whilst you're out tomorrow," Hilda sighed.

"And not just biscuits and tea. I mean proper meals," her Mum warned.

"Damn, my plan has been foiled!" Hilda sarcastically commented.

"How's the writing coming along?" her Mum asked, swiftly changing the subject.

"I finally wrote something last night," Hilda replied. "It's coming along, but it's only the first draft of a short story. It still needs to take proper shape as it were."

"A first draft is better than nothing at all, love," Her Mum told her. "Keep at it!" Her Mum left the hallway to go downstairs. Hilda shut the door to her bedroom. She went back to her laptop and continued browsing for jobs.

Chapter Eighteen

Leaf sank slowly back to the ground of the church. She was still surrounded by crosses and candles as she hit the ground. Vikram looked on, impressed.

"That was spectacular," Vikram commented. "Did it work though?"

"I don't know. I think so. I felt that surge of energy, so I hope that means it worked," Leaf wondered. Suddenly, the door flew open. Rex and his three vampire lackeys came charging through the open door. The vampires immediately crowded Vikram. Leaf stood quickly as she prepared to face off with Rex. She was conflicted on whether to focus on Rex or an outnumbered Vikram.

"Only get him if he moves!" Rex commanded his trio. He faced a worried Leaf. Vikram was surrounded by the trio of vampire disciples. He knew that one wrong move would've led to a difficult fight for him.

"If he makes one false move, I'll command my men to eat him alive," Rex warned Leaf. "You can either come with me or both of you die. Your choice." Leaf turned to face Vikram, who nodded slightly to her. Leaf turned back to Rex angrily.

"If he's killed, I'll kill you," Leaf threatened Rex.

"I'm offering a one time deal here," Rex continued, "Something to really consider." Leaf wanted to throttle Rex for his comment but didn't want to get Vikram killed. She stepped out of the holy cross and candle circle. Rex put his arm around Leaf.

"I'm not so bad, y'know," Rex whispered in Leaf's ear. "You'll understand just like your sister does." Leaf wanted to back away from Rex, but he held onto her with his vampire-strength grip. He dragged her away from Vikram, who was still surrounded by the vampire servants. Rex took Leaf out the door and towards the stage. Leaf tripped up. Sensing resistance, Rex pulled at her hair and pulled her the rest of the way to the stage.

"Bloody hell, I tripped up," Leaf protested.

"No more out of your mouth," Rex spat as he continued to pull Leaf to the stage. They got on the stage to meet a seemingly composed but slightly dazed Regina. Rex threw Leaf to the ground of the stage. He turned to face his remaining loyalists.

"My friends, we have a treat for you," Rex began to tell his fans, "Not only is this woman a witch, but a part of the resistance who just surrendered to me." The vampires in the crowd cheered. Leaf started to raise her head to face her sister. Before she could do anything, Rex picked her up by the scruff of her neck and presented her to the vampire hoard.

"This witch has been a thorn in my side ever since I came here. Have fun with her but don't eat. There's plenty of fun you can have with a woman like this!" Rex bragged. He dangled Leaf over the edge of the stage as the vampires gathered around her, desperate to get a piece of her. Regina snapped out of her daze, realising her sister was in grave danger. Leaf started to chant under her breath. Rex pulled her in to try to hear her.

"What's the little witch trying to say?" Rex taunted. Leaf finished chanting. Her clothes started to burn Rex's hand. He dropped her back onto the floor of the stage. His hands were smoking from the effect of her spell. The vampire group were shocked at what they'd seen. The human group saw their opportunity and started to run.

"Get those humans!" Rex yelled at his followers. They started to go after them. Leaf looked up from her position. She stuck out her right hand, aiming at the group of fleeing humans.

"Nolite lamia!" Leaf screamed. The group of vampires were stopped in their tracks. They turned and ran back to Rex at the stage. He grabbed Leaf again, angry at her defiance.

"You will pay for this, you wretched fool!" Rex screamed at Leaf. He turned her to face him. Just as he was about to bite her, she was tackled away by Regina. Rex and the vampire group turned to face Regina and Leaf. Rex was in shock for a moment.

"Stay down," Regina whispered in Leaf's ear. Regina got up to face Rex.

"My Queen, don't -" Rex started.

"I'm not your Queen anymore," Regina snarled, "You will not hurt her."

Chapter Nineteen

It was the following Friday evening in the Leaf household. Hilda was sitting in her bedroom on the laptop, writing. She took a break to look around her room, which was very much empty with exception to the furniture. It crept her out a bit how bare it felt. Only that morning it was her regular bedroom. Now it was an empty husk of what it once was. There was very little left that really made the room Hilda's in her eyes. It felt like a spare room in her Mum's home. She stood in her room, continuing to feel uneasy. She decided to leave her bedroom and head down to the nearby beach whilst there was still sunlight. She grabbed her phone and headphones, ran down the stairs, grabbed her shoes, and put them on. She grabbed her keys and put her phone in her pocket. She went out the door and locked it behind her. She put on her headphones and put on some Blackbeard's Tea Party on her music app. As she got closer to the beach, she started to feel more relaxed, feeling the wind. She sat on the bench closer to the pebbles of the beach. She saw many people walk by: parents collecting their children to go home, elderly couples taking in a walk together, and individuals walking their energetic dogs. Over her headphones, she could hear the sound of people walking on the beach, their passing conversations, and the sound of the sea crashing onto the pebbles underneath. She sat back and stared out to the sea. She concentrated on the tide coming in and out. She didn't even notice Jack approaching her from the side. He sat next to her. She turned and had a fright seeing him there.

"Sorry. I know you hate being touched unexpectedly," Jack apologised. Hilda turned off her music and headphones. She faced Jack.

"It's okay. What are you doing here?" Hilda asked politely.

"After I finished work, I wanted to see if you needed any help with packing. I went to your place, but no one was home," Jack explained.

"Mum's gone to get the moving lorry. How did you figure out where I was?"

"I know you like to wander where there are the least amount of people around. I know the nearby park has that fair in town, so I figured you'd be here instead."

"You know me well," Hilda said, smiling at him. She kissed him on the lips. He kissed her back.

"Was that okay? I know we hadn't discussed public displays of affection," Hilda asked, worried she'd done the wrong thing. Jack smiled at her.

"I didn't hate it," Jack coolly told her. He reached out and held Hilda's hand. She felt a rush of excitement as he touched her. They looked each other in the eye and smiled. Hilda started to blush. Jack noticed.

"What's up?" Jack asked.

"Nothing?" Hilda hesitated. "Okay, I'm just a bit excited. I mean, I've never had anyone hold my hand in public before like this. Don't get me wrong: it's hardly like I'm some sort of sexual virgin, but I'm definitely a bit of a relationship virgin."

Jack giggled slightly.

"I know. It's okay," Jack reassured her, "It's very cute."

"I just have to make sure we don't start to move too quickly," Hilda warned. "I want to still take things one step at a time."

"I know, Hilda. I'd rather we took our time, too," Jack agreed. "At least when you decide you're ready, we'll be ready." Jack looked at the time on his watch: it was 7:30pm.

"Do you want to head back to the house?" Jack asked Hilda. Hilda looked out to the sea. The sun was starting to truly set. She smiled at the beautiful colours in the sky. She faced Jack again.

"Shall we just sit together for a little while and enjoy the sunset?" Hilda proposed. Jack let go of her hand and put his arm around her. Hilda placed her head on his shoulder. She felt content to look at the sunset in Jack's loving embrace.

Jack and Hilda arrived back at Hilda's home three quarters of an hour later. They got into the house and locked the door behind them. Hilda wiped her feet four times each. Jack and Hilda faced each other longingly. They went in for a kiss. At first it was tender, but then it skyrocketed into a passionate frenzy. Their hands were all over each other, clinging to each other. Just as they were about to head upstairs, they heard the door unlock. They separated from each other and quickly composed themselves. Hilda's Mum came through the door. She was surprised to see Hilda and Jack together.

"Hello, love," her Mum greeted her.

"Hi, Mum," Hilda responded, still blushing somewhat, "Did you get the lorry okay?"

"Yes, I did. How're you Jack?" Hilda's Mum greeted Jack.

"I'm good thanks, Ms. Leaf." Jack politely returned the greeting.

"You can call me Matilda," Hilda's Mum nudged Jack gently. "Are you going to stay for dinner?"

"Only if that's okay?" Jack accepted tentatively.

"Absolutely. I've got quite a lot of rice. Who fancies some chicken curry?" Hilda's Mum proposed to the pair.

"That'll be great. Thanks Mum!" Hilda enthusiastically agreed. Her Mum went into the kitchen. Jack and Hilda breathed a sigh of relief.

"I suppose that could've gone worse," Jack commented.

"She's not stupid Jack," Hilda argued. "She clearly knows what we were doing."

"Oh I know," Jack continued. "At least we weren't butt naked doing anything that may have scarred her for life."

"I suppose," Hilda relented. "Although now I'm all bothered with nothing to do about it." She went in for another kiss. They kissed but Jack broke away.

"There'll be plenty of time to do that tomorrow after we're done moving your things," Jack compromised with Hilda. She smiled at him.

"Why don't you wait in the living room? I'm going to see if Mum needs any help," Hilda suggested. He went to sit in the living room whilst she went into the kitchen. She stood by the kitchen doorway to see her Mum preparing the chicken.

"Mum, do you need any help?" Hilda asked. Her Mum turned to face her.

"I'm fine, love," she replied. "Why don't you and Jack watch some tv whilst I cook?" Hilda's Mum turned to prepare the chicken again. Hilda hovered by the door.

"Mum," Hilda asked, "You're not mad at me, are you?" Hilda's Mum faced her again.

"Why would I be mad at you?" she asked.

"Jack's here and I didn't ask ahead and we weren't just chatting innocently before you turned up," Hilda blurted out.

"Again, why would I be mad? As long as you and Jack aren't doing anything wrong I don't see why I should be mad," her Mum reassured her. "Besides, Jack's a nice boy. He'll be a good boyfriend once things have settled down with you."

Hilda smiled at her.

"You mean that?"

"Of course I do. I would hug you but I'm handling raw chicken. I'll give you a hug later, okay?"

"Okay. Love you, Mum."

"Love you, too."

Three in the morning on Saturday slowly crept in. Hilda was unable to sleep next to her lover, Jack, who was sound asleep. She got up quietly and sat on the edge of her bed. She contemplated what she was going to do. She'd packed away her laptop earlier in the evening so she couldn't resort to writing into the morning hours. She decided to head down the stairs and watch some television quietly until her Mum and Jack woke up in a few hours. She crept quietly down the stairs and made her way into the living room. She was surprised to see her Mum sitting already watching the news on the television.

"Mum?" Hilda called out to her Mum. She turned to face Hilda.

"Hilda! What are you doing up so late?" her Mum asked.

"I could ask you the same thing, Mum," Hilda retorted.

"I couldn't sleep," her Mum admitted.

"Why?" Hilda asked curiously.

"This is going to be harder than I thought it would be," her Mum sighed, "Don't get me wrong: I want you to move into Kate's old flat so you can have your own space. It'll be good for you. I'll just feel a bit lonely here in the house alone." Hilda went to sit next to her Mum. She hesitantly put her hand on her Mum's shoulder. She then took her hand away.

"I don't have to move," Hilda offered, "I could always sell the flat."

"I don't want that for you. I can't use my selfish desire to keep you here," her Mum rejected Hilda's offer. "You need to take this opportunity to live your life independently. You could really thrive." Her Mum put her arm around Hilda, who shuffled uncomfortably.

"I only want what's best for you, Hilda," her Mum concluded.

"I know."

"Besides, at least this way you can really get some privacy with Jack without coordinating around my schedule."

"That's true. I will miss seeing you every day, Mum."

"I'll miss you, too. We can always text each other. It doesn't have to be every day, but we can keep in touch."

"That'll be nice."

"I promise I will do my best not to hassle you."

"Thanks, Mum." Hilda and her Mum turned to face the television. They both tried to concentrate on the content of the news.

"What's going on in the world? I feel like I've been disconnected lately..." Hilda asked her Mum.

"Oh God, I don't know. I haven't really been paying attention," her Mum admitted, "I think some person is pushing another crappy legislation with very little opposition again."

"So business as usual?" Hilda summed up.

"Pretty much," her Mum agreed with her. "I'm going to go back to bed. Try to get some sleep, love." Her Mum stood up and left the room to head back up the stairs to her bedroom. Hilda stayed on the sofa and continued to watch the 24-hour news channel, hoping to bore herself to sleep. She stayed up for a few more moments, keeping an eye on the time as she did. Before she knew it, it was 4am. She felt irritated that she still wasn't sleepy. She started to browse the channels on the television until she gave up and turned the tv off. She decided to try to get some sleep. She went back up the stairs into her bedroom. She smiled as she saw a still-sleeping Jack in her bed. She slipped quietly and easily into her bed and cuddled up to Jack. She started to finally fall asleep.

Chapter Twenty

Regina stood tall as Rex went up to her and tried to touch her face. She battered him away aggressively. Rex was visibly confused. He turned to face his vampire followers who looked confused and put off by what was transpiring in front of them. Rex turned angrily back to Regina.

"I don't know what you're doing but cut it out," Rex fiercely barked at Regina.

"I won't let you hurt her or anyone else," Regina fired back at him. He tried to go for Leaf, who was staying down on the ground, but Regina stopped him and threw him off the stage and across the parkland. He hit a tree before hitting the ground. He quickly got back up, flustered. He tried to compose himself quickly. Leaf started to get up, supported by Regina. The vampire group, now disinterested, started to leave. Rex began to realise he'd lost his psychological grip on Regina. He charged back towards the stage.

"You'll pay for this!" Rex screamed as he started to go after Leaf. Regina stopped him by pushing Leaf away and kicking Rex hard in the face. This hurtled him away from the stage again.

"You'll pay for this!" Rex snarled as he walked away from the stage area, into the night. Regina turned to face Leaf.

"Are you okay?" Regina asked a shocked Leaf.

"I'm okay," Leaf answered. Leaf approached Regina, but Regina stepped away from Leaf.

"Are you okay?" Leaf sputtered. Regina shook her head. Leaf tried to reach out to her sister, but she rejected her touch.

"Are you mad at me?" Leaf asked dejectedly.

"It's complicated, Leaf," Regina finally spoke again. "I appreciate what you were trying to do, but now I have to live with this soul. I have to live with the bad things I've done and feel bad about it."

"We can work through this together," Leaf tried to reassure her, but Regina turned away from her.

"I have to do this alone," Regina said. Before Leaf could respond, Regina ran away, breaking Leaf's heart in the process. The rejection was overwhelming for her. She crumbled onto the stage crying. She felt so dejected by her sister's reaction. She hadn't anticipated it. She tried to compose herself, but struggled to pull herself together as she sobbed. A moment later, she felt a hand on her shoulder. She turned, ready for a fight, only to find Vikram behind her. She got up from the ground, shocked to see him not only alive but fine.

"Are you -?" Vikram started. He was interrupted by Leaf clinging to him, crying. Vikram held onto her, giving her the space to express her sadness.

The morning dawned across the Brighthelmston skies. Vikram and Leaf came through to the county hospital's intensive care unit. Argus was awake, but visibly in pain and uncomfortable. The sounds of machines beeping took up the atmosphere in the room. Leaf and Vikram surrounded his bed. Leaf held his unbroken hand.

"Hey," Leaf greeted Argus. "How're you feeling today?"

"Leaf," Argus croaked, "You're here."

"Yeah. I'm here," Leaf repeated.

"You were right, Argus - she managed to stop Rex in the way she planned," Vikram told him. Argus squeezed Leaf's hand gently.

"I knew you'd get it done," Argus told Leaf.

"He's still out there. He'll pop up again," Leaf said, feeling deflated.

"It's okay, we'll get him," Vikram tried to comfort her. Leaf sighed.

"Regina walked away from me, Argus. I don't think she'll forgive me," Leaf lamented.

"She'll get there. She just needs time to adjust," Vikram tried to reassure her. Leaf turned to face Vikram. She half-smiled, then turned back to Argus.

"How long do they reckon you'll be here?" Leaf asked Argus.

"They can't say," Argus quietly explained, "Hopefully soon," Leaf held onto his hand.

"I'm just relieved you're alive. Don't scare me like that again," said Leaf.

"I'll do my best," Argus croaked. Leaf and Vikram stayed a while whilst Argus rested a bit more.

Chapter Twenty-One

It was the following Saturday at 8am. Hilda's alarm on her phone started to sound off. She grabbed her phone and turned off the alarm. Jack started to get up, refreshed from his sleep. Hilda grabbed her covers, hiding her face into them. She grumbled, having not had a huge amount of sleep. Jack turned to face Hilda.

"Wake up, silly monkey," Jack teased Hilda, "We've got to get ready to move your things to your flat." He tried to pry the covers from over Hilda's face, but her grip was too strong. Jack smirked. He got under the covers and started to tickle Hilda. She let go of the covers, giggling away as Jack continued to tickle her all over her torso. He took the opportunity to grab the covers and took them away from Hilda.

"That was wicked," Hilda complained through giggles.

"You're laughing, therefore you can't be mad," Jack teased her. "Besides, we need to wake up and help your Mum."

"I suppose," Hilda relented. She started to get up from her bed. She turned to face Jack.

"I'm out of bed now. Are you happy now?" Hilda said to Jack. Jack was lying to his side with a big grin on his face.

"I just wanted you to wake up. I didn't say you had to get up just yet," Jack cheekily remarked. Hilda half-smiled back at him. She got back into her bed. She kissed him on the lips.

"You're so cute," Hilda complimented him.

"I know," Jack replied. They kissed each other tenderly. They were getting lost in each other when they heard a knock on the door.

"Hilda, love, are you up?" Hilda's Mum questioned through the door.

"Yeah," Hilda replied.

"I'll pop the kettle on to make a cup of tea. Do you both want one?" her Mum asked.

"Yes, please!" Jack and Hilda replied in unison.

"Okay, come down when you're ready," her Mum said as she walked away and down the stairs. Jack and Hilda faced each other.

"We'd better get dressed," Hilda sighed.

It was an hour later. Hilda, her Mum, and Jack were picking up boxes of Hilda's stuff. They took them out into the lorry Hilda's Mum had hired. They placed the boxes carefully into the lorry. Once all the boxes were in there, they placed a suitcase each of clothes into the lorry. Jack closed the doors. Hilda and her Mum faced each other.

"Are you ready to go?" her Mum asked her, placing her arm around her daughter. Hilda turned to face her childhood home. She was full of mixed emotions. She was saying goodbye to the home she'd grown up in, but she felt like it was the right time in her life to do this.

"Yeah. Let's go," Hilda resolved. Her Mum squeezed her arm. She took her arm away and started to get into the lorry. Hilda turned to Jack.

"I think there's only two seats in the lorry," Jack told her. "If you can text me the address, I'll meet you there."

"Okay," Hilda agreed. She kissed him on the cheek. Jack left. Hilda got into the moving lorry, sitting next to her Mum.

"He's going to meet us there," Hilda said.

"Okay. Let's get moving," her Mum started the moving lorry. The lorry started smoothly without a judder or a pause. Her Mum started the fifteen minute drive to Hilda's flat. Hilda texted Jack the address as her Mum drove. She put her phone away.

"How're you feeling, love?" Hilda's Mum asked.

"I'm okay, Mum." Hilda said passively.

"Are you sure you're not just saying that?" Her Mum grilled.

"I'm fine, Mum. It's just going to be an adjustment," Hilda admitted, "I think you were right last night: this will be good for my sense of independence."

"You'll see, love, that having your own space will be really good for you," her Mum assured her. Hilda turned to see the sea go by as they drove along the coastal road. She was caught up in the waxing and waning sea tide, the still pebbles of the beach, and the people walking by. As they turned away from the coastal road towards her new flat, Hilda felt a sense of both trepidation and excitement. She was surprised to feel the excitement. After all, this was a major change and she didn't deal well with change usually. They arrived a few minutes later at the flat complex. Her Mum pulled up into a loading bay. She pulled the brake and parked. She turned to face Hilda.

"We're here, love," said Hilda's Mum. Hilda looked at the flat building. It was an unassuming brown brick building with white mini balconies at the front. She unbuckled her seat belt, carefully got out of the lorry, and took out her flat keys. She walked onto the pavement next to her flat building; looking up again, she smiled.

It was 9pm. The darkness descended upon the Brighton skies. Hilda sat alone in her new living room. She was unsure of what to do. She was still adjusting to her new environment. She looked around. She felt a little uneasy now that she was on her own. She got up from her sofa and looked around at the walls. Her sister's old DSLR camera was hanging by its strap near the television. She smiled at the old DSLR camera as she felt as if an element of her sister remained in the flat beyond her remaining furniture. She looked around again at her surroundings.

"Well, this is mine now," Hilda thought to herself. She wandered into the kitchen. She got out a loaf of sliced tiger bread. As she waited for her bread to toast, she tapped her fingers on the kitchen counter in a funky rhythm. Her toast sprung from the toaster. She grabbed it, placed some butter on it, and started to eat. She was enjoying herself with her toast when she heard her phone go off. She rushed to answer her phone.

"Hello?" Hilda answered.

"Hi, is this Hilda Leaf?" the voice on the other side of the phone spoke.

"Yes?" Hilda said hesitantly.

"I'm Marjorie Ziff, the office manager for the Calm Way therapy office," Marjorie introduced herself, "You applied for the Receptionist job in Brighton a couple of days ago. Are you still interested?"

"Yes, I am," Hilda replied enthusiastically.

"I'd like to bring you in for an interview. Are you available on Monday morning?" Marjorie enquired.

"Yeah, I'm free whenever you are," Hilda responded.

"Great. Shall we say 9am?"

"Absolutely. I'll see you then."

"Fantastic. I'll send you the details tomorrow. Sorry to have called at such a late hour."

"That's okay. I'll see you on Monday." Hilda hung up the phone with a smile on her face. She felt a sense of hope that she was truly rebuilding her life.

It was 9am the next morning. Hilda woke up with a start. She was alarmed by her new surroundings. It took a hot second to remember where she was and the events of the past day. She sighed out of relief and frustration with herself for scaring herself like that. She got up from her new double bed and went to her bathroom. She began brushing her teeth. As she did, she heard her phone start to go off. She quickly finished brushing, spat out the toothpaste, put the toothbrush down and ran into her bedroom. She just missed the call. As she picked up her phone, it started ringing again. It was her Mum. Worried, she answered it.

"Hi, Mum," Hilda answered, worried, "Is everything okay?"

"Yes, everything is fine, love. I just wanted to check in and make sure you're okay," Her Mum answered honestly.

"Oh," Hilda said as she felt relief wave over her, "I'm okay, Mum. Are you okay?"

"I'm fine," her Mum replied. "How're you finding it, being on your own over there?" Hilda thought about it for a moment.

"It's an adjustment. I'll get there, though," Hilda told her Mum.

"Oh good, I'm glad to hear that," her Mum replied happily, "Did you get any writing done?"

"I only just got up, Mum. I'll probably do some later." Hilda said.

"Okay, love. I'll let you get on with it. I love you," her Mum told her daughter.

"I love you too, Mum," Hilda reciprocated. They both hung up on each other. Hilda decided to get dressed. She got into her underwear, a pun t-shirt, and colourful trousers. She got into her sandals. She grabbed her trusted satchel bag, phone and headphones. She put on her headphones and turned on some music on her phone. She grabbed her flat keys, left, and locked the door behind her. She wandered away from her flat building towards the seaside a few moments away. As she did, she thought about everything in the past few weeks that had led to this point. She thought about her previous job, her relationship with Kate, and the way she lost both. She went through every little action, every single thing she said, every possible scenario that didn't happen but could've in her mind. She felt anxiety in her heart over what could've been, had she actually done something different. She walked faster towards the beach view as she saw it come over the horizon. The thoughts were circling and clouding her mind: what if I hadn't left the room when Kate lashed out? What if I had just kept my mouth shut to Mrs. Walton? What if I was different and could handle either situation better? What if I wasn't autistic? Everything seemed to come to a stop once she reached the side of the road closest to the sea. She looked out to the wide ocean upon the horizon. She felt more at ease the longer she looked at it. The whirling thoughts started to dissipate. She felt a sense of certainty as she looked at the waning sea – a sense of calm, assurance, and peace. She looked at her hands as she placed them on the pavement rail separating her from the sharp drop to the beach below. She looked back to the sea. Whilst she knew Kate was long gone, she felt her presence almost comfort her in a way she'd seldom felt before. She smiled, closed her eyes, and embraced the moment whilst it lasted before she opened her eyes, let go of the rail, and walked away.

About the author

Jennifer Drewett is an author who writes about polyamory, neurodiversity, LGBTQ+ issues, or as she puts it 'interesting people'. She has written articles for The Cosplay Journal and We Make Movies on Weekends.

She's been a writer for years having written articles, novels, and essays. Working a part time job in the NHS, she spends her free time looking for the next story.

She has an official website: www.jenniferdrewett.com.